"I have admired Miss Drabble's writing for years. . . . Like Doris Lessing, she has that genius of the forcefully 'creating' work of fiction . . . a total mastery of the mysterious form of the novel." —Joyce Carol Oates

"Impressive. . . . Here is a writer of real intelligence, using the English language with precision but without affectation, and shaping words and plot to a clear purpose." —*Times Literary Supplement*

"A lady of awesome talent." —*The Wall Street Journal*

MARGARET DRABBLE is the author of *The Millstone, The Middle Ground, The Realms of Gold, The Needle's Eye*, and other novels, as well as a biography of Arnold Bennett. She lives in London with her three children.

The Garrick Year

Margaret Drabble

A PLUME BOOK

NEW AMERICAN LIBRARY

NEW YORK AND SCARBOROUGH, ONTARIO

For Adam and Angela

NAL BOOKS ARE AVAILABLE AT QUANTITY DISCOUNTS
WHEN USED TO PROMOTE PRODUCTS OR SERVICES.
FOR INFORMATION PLEASE WRITE TO
PREMIUM MARKETING DIVISION,
NEW AMERICAN LIBRARY, 1633 BROADWAY,
NEW YORK, NEW YORK 10019.

Published by arrangement with
William Morrow & Company, Inc.

 PLUME TRADEMARK REG. U.S. PAT. OFF. AND FOREIGN COUNTRIES
REGISTERED TRADEMARK—MARCA REGISTRADA
HECHO EN HARRISONBURG, VA., U.S.A.

SIGNET, SIGNET CLASSIC, MENTOR, PLUME, ME-
RIDIAN and NAL BOOKS are published *in the United
States* by New American Library, 1633 Broadway, New
York, New York 10019, *in Canada* by The New American
Library of Canada Limited, 81 Mack Avenue, Scarborough,
Ontario M1L 1M8

Cover painting, "Jeune fille à la fenêtre", by Balthus.
© SPADEM, Paris/VAGA, New York, 1984.

Library of Congress Catalog Card Number: 84-60620

First Plume Printing, August, 1984

1 2 3 4 5 6 7 8 9

PRINTED IN THE UNITED STATES OF AMERICA

1

WHILE I was watching the advertisements on television last night, I saw Sophy Brent. I have not set eyes on her for some months, and the sight of her filled me with a curious warm mixture of nostalgia and amusement. She was, typically enough, eating: she was advertising a new kind of chocolate cake, and the picture showed her in a shining kitchen gazing in rapture at this cake, then cutting a slice and raising it to her moist, curved, delightful lips. There the picture ended. It would not have done to show the public the crumbs and the chewing. I was very excited by this fleeting glimpse, as I always am by the news of old friends, and it aroused in me a whole flood of recollections, recollections of Sophy herself, and of all that strange season, that Garrick year, as I shall always think of it, which proved to me to be such a turning point, though from what to what I would hardly like to say.

Poor old Sophy, I allowed myself to say, thinking that she would not much like being on a cake advertisement; and then I remembered the last time I had said Poor old Sophy, and that in any case, she would have earned a lot of money from that tantalizing moment. There is perhaps something finally unpitiable in Sophy, just as there is in me. We are both in our ways excellent examples of resilience, though I seem obliged to pass through many alienating degrees of meanness on my way, whereas she just smiles and wriggles and exclaims and with a little charming confusion gets by. I like Sophy. I cannot help liking Sophy. And if there is a defensive note to be detected in that assertion, I am not in the least surprised.

That chocolate cake vision made me think back, as I said, over the whole lot, right back to the very beginning, to the occasion when I first realized that David was really intending to go to Hereford. I had just finished putting Flora to bed, and I came downstairs, splashed and bedraggled from her bath, to find David nursing the new baby and drinking a glass of beer. He had poured some stout for me, which was the only thing he would let me drink. When I appeared he handed the baby over quickly, and as I sat down and prepared to feed him, wondering if I would ever get him to wake at a less exhausting time, Dave spoke.

"Wyndham sent me the script for Edmund Carpenter's new play," he said.

I listened to this statement as the tiny, mousy, pathetic scrap of child latched itself onto my breast: I must, I said to myself, keep calm, or the child will get wind and I will be feeding him all night.

"Oh yes," I said after a while. "Is it a good play?"

"It's all right," he said. "It's a very good part."

"Which part?"

"Now look here, Emma," said David, and

at his tone I bent my face all the more intently away from him and towards my baby, "I don't honestly see what I can do about it. We've got to go, and that's that. It's only for seven months, and you'll bloody well have to lump it. I can't afford not to go."

"What do you mean," I said, "you can't afford not to go? You told me last week you were rolling in money. And I thought you were signed up to do that television next month."

"I can do that as well," said David.

"Well, in that case," I said, hearing with alarm in my own voice a tone threatening imminent disaster, "you'll be able to afford anything you want, won't you?"

"It isn't a question of money," he said, and out rolled those classic, inevitable words once more, "it's a question of my career."

"Really, Dave my darling," I said with the unnatural evenness demanded by the quiet, even sucking, "I think your career is perfectly all right without your hopping off to the wilds of the country to some artsy festival where they'll probably pay you fifteen pounds a week and expect you to be grateful."

"Wyndham mentioned a salary," he said with that smug look that had been possessing him lately.

"And what about me?" I said querulously, knowing that I had lost as soon as I realized that the economics of the scheme had met with David's approval and would therefore certainly meet with mine. "What about me? I'd got everything so tidily arranged, I can't just mess it all up again to go trailing all over England after you, can I?"

"Of course you can," he said. "Anyway, it isn't a question of all over England, it would be Hereford, for seven months. We can let this place and take a house there, and you'll have Pascal to help you with everything. It would be very good for you and the babies. I wouldn't ask you to go just anywhere, but the country's good for you."

"Good for me! Good for me!" I exclaimed with fury, and at my violence the baby unclasped himself and started to cry. I sat him up and patted his back, and tried for his sake to be calm again. "Look," I said to David, "why don't we leave this little chat until I've finished feeding Joe? It's not worth upsetting him, I'll be here all evening if we go on like this. Why don't you leave me alone for half an hour, and then we can begin again?"

"I'll leave you for the night if you want," he said, getting up and finishing his beer. "But there won't be any point in beginning again. I signed the contract this morning." And thereupon he walked out.

Poor Joseph imbibed a good deal of bile along with his milk that evening. I subsequently found out that what Dave had said about the contract was not in fact true. He had not signed it, as I should have suspected at the time, and did not do so until he had dragged a formal approval out of me. On the other hand, the determination that I had recognized in him had been quite real, and what was my determination against his? There was nothing I could say or do to deflect him. I thought that he might have had the fairness to wait until Joseph's feed was over before raising the sub-

ject: our tempers are evenly matched, and we
usually conduct our discussions with equal
virulence, but one is at a hopeless disadvantage
with a baby on one's knee, with milk dripping
all over and the prospect of a sleepless night
if one loses one's temper. It is too much to expect of other people that they will remember
such conditions. I do not expect it, but on the
other hand, I cannot behave as though they
have remembered. So my behaviour is ruined,
even while I try to preserve my judgment. I
often think that motherhood, in its physical aspects, is like one of those trying disorders such
as hay fever or asthma, which receive verbal
sympathy but no real consideration, in view of
their lack of fatality, and which, after years of
attrition, can sour and pervert the character
beyond all recovery. Motherhood has of course
infinite compensations, though I can well believe that some people are driven to a point
where they cannot feel them.

I must say, however, that even if David had
waited like a politician for a promising moment
to approach me, he could hardly have found
one. I was very unapproachable at that time,
and I found the idea of going to Hereford peculiarly upsetting. I had been promised a couple of months before a very pleasant job as a
newsreader and announcer by a television company which had decided, as such companies
will, to have another attempt at the equality
of the sexes by allowing women to announce
serious events as well as forthcoming pro-
grammes. I was to have been a pioneer in this
field, and I fully expected to succeed where
others had failed. The job, admittedly, had

been procured for me by an old friend and admirer, for whom I used to do a little sporadic
fashion modelling before my marriage, but despite this string-pulling everyone admitted that
I was admirably suited for such a post. I have
a face of quite startling and effective gravity, a
pure accident of feature, I believe, and people
automatically trust what I say. The nation
would have been impressed by the news as
read by me. And I for my part would have
enjoyed reading it: I have always had a passion
for facts and a mild yearning for notoriety, and
I could imagine no more happy way of com-
bining these two interests. And after three
years of childbearing and modelling maternity
clothes, I felt in serious need of a good, steady,
lucrative job.

I could hardly believe that marriage was going to deprive me of this, too. It had already
deprived me of so many things which I had
childishly overvalued: my independence, my
income, my twenty-two-inch waist, my sleep,
most of my friends, who had deserted on account of David's insults, a whole string of finite things, and many more indefinite attributes, like hope and expectation. And now,
just when I had got my future organized and
had glimpsed, as it were, the end of solitude,
I had been pushed right back to where I had
started. There seemed to be no answer but
stoicism, a philosophy which I find I can practice, but which I neither enjoy nor admire.

I got Joe to bed after half an hour more of
feeding; he was far too small to notice my
mood, fortunately, though he did wake up later
with wind. Then I went downstairs again and

walked up and down the living room and thought. I thought about Hereford, and David's career, and Wyndham Farrar. I had met Wyndham Farrar only once in my life before, though naturally I knew all about him, as did anyone who was connected with the theatre. And may I make it clear that I was connected only by marriage, I have no aspirations in that direction myself, though I have aspirations towards gloss, which can be mistaken for the same thing. Wyndham Farrar, in any case, was a name which one could not fail to recognize. He was a director, and everything he did, good or bad, achieved a certain distinction: he was a free-lancer, and had never associated himself with any of the trends or mass managements of the theatre, but would turn up from time to time in unexpected countries with unexpected plays, the odd bad film or good television production, and so on. Most people seemed to have worked with him at some time or another, and everyone spoke of him either with awe or admiration. I could never work out whether he was what in the theatre passes for an intellectual, or whether he was simply a misfit, or whether he had enough private means not to have to work in the usual humdrum West End, television contract fashion. However he had done it, he had managed to make himself accepted as some sort of important and unpredictable figure, whose moves were always worth following and whose judgement was always of interest; and certainly the first time I met him I noticed him as one would notice a significant person. I went out of my way at this meeting not to be noticed by him, as I

was very pregnant at the time: it was just before Joe was born. But I paid attention.

It was at a party that this meeting took place;
the party was given by a rather classy television director, for whom David had just played
a flashy and well-paid role, and it took place
in a top-story flat in Hampstead, with the most
miraculous falling, fading view from its windows. David and I were just chatting with this
man's wife, a lady in purple trousers, when
Wyndham Farrar approached us; I recognized
him because I had seen him on television the
week before talking about the theatre in the
provinces, in some programme on the arts.
What a world it is, where everyone's face is
continually before one, the loved and the forgotten and the about-to-be-loved, all there,
falsely thrust upon one's memory every night of
the week. No wonder that I wanted to get my
face on that dark receiving box myself, to join
that intricate pattern, the celluloid drama
that is played out there every night at the dis-
cretion of the programme arrangers: Sophy
Brent and Wyndham Farrar and David Evans,
my husband, and that bland-faced woman that
should have been me.

Wyndham looked better in real life than on
film, unlike my handsome husband: his face
had seemed too large and shapeless for the
screen, but in the flesh it had a bashed-about,
deeply folded vigour and its shapelessness
seemed to have planes of complexity which the
camera had not shown. He was the same height
as David, which is not as high by an inch as
me, and thickset; one might say even fat, had
he not been so broadly built. He had a thor-

oughgoing masculinity: his whole shape lacked any attempt at grace, and his clothes hung on him coarsely like appendages. He was the other end of the scale from our host, who was a long-shanked, carefully dressed, delicate gentleman. I preferred the look of Wyndham, who came up to us and said to this man's wife, with the broad, self-possessed complacency of importance:

"Hello, Kate. Introduce me to this clever young man, will you?"

The wife introduced David and, inevitably, me. Wyndham did not so much as cast a glance in my direction, except when he took my hand: his eyes swept perfunctorily over my form and left it at that. I did not blame him. I would have done the same myself. I knew that I was disqualified. He congratulated David on his performance in this woman's husband's play, and they talked about it a little. Then Wyndham said:

"What about coming to Hereford with me next year?"

"What for?" said David.

"Oh, for the Festival," said Wyndham. "Didn't you know about the Festival? A nice new theatre I'm going to have, and if I get my own way I'm going to do some nice interesting plays. I can even think of a line of parts waiting for you. You're just the kind of person we want down there."

"Oh well," said David, "I haven't been on the stage for years."

"You're not so old," said Wyndham. "And don't you feel the call of all those live audiences?"

"Will they be very live in Hereford? I can't say I do, really. I quite like things as they are."

"Do you? Don't you feel the signs of acting in a vacuum?"

"Anyway, I think I'm doing a film next year," said David. He did not think anything of the kind, but he was always saying things like that. And so he and Wyndham left it. The project seemed sufficiently vague for me to feel it wiser not to intervene, and in any case, I knew David would be quite clear about where I stood on the subject: the provinces have never appealed to me, except as curiosities. But being clear about my position has never influenced David as much as I think it should, so being aware of this, I did a little investigation of my own about the Hereford scheme, to which stray references grew sadly thicker in the succeeding weeks. It appeared that a new theatre was being built there, and that Wyndham Farrar was to open it next spring with a season of plays. With his sanction, the whole affair would obviously be a classy, well-financed occasion, not a dutiful pinch and scrape. The names of various prominent artists had already been mentioned in connection with it, and at least twenty-five percent of them would probably go. I had not seriously intended my crack about the fifteen pounds a week salary: I knew that David would be able to get more than that out of them. But on the other hand, our standard of expenditure was so absurdly high that we would need more than any straight classical work out of London or indeed in it would be likely to bring. I cannot think what we spent our money on: the mortgage of the house, I suppose, which was the only sensible project I ever persuaded him to undertake, and the usual wasteful nonsense of clothes and drinks and ridiculous toys and excursions. I mean excursions, not holidays: we never went away, but we spent a fortune on days at the zoo, in Brighton, on river trips, in weekend hotels of vast luxury. For someone not born to money David certainly knows how to spend: he is wonderfully extravagant, and has no idea of saving or of value. Compared with him I am as mean as hell; he was brought up in poverty and I in professional comfort, and this may have something to do with it. He used to shock me at times, with his taxis and his double whiskies. I wondered what would happen to him if he had to do without. I am always trying to do without, just to practice, just in case, and this annoys him; it is sad to see how often in a domestic situation one's virtues can become a curse. His extravagance is one of the things in him that I have always loved.

You see now perhaps a selection of the reasons for which I so opposed the idea of going to Hereford. I thought them over to myself as I waited for David to come back. He never walked out for long, though he was quick to go. My strongest reason, I must admit, was that I could not bear to relinquish the idea of this television job that I had acquired: it seemed such a perfect answer to everything, as it involved a good, steady wage and only three afternoons and evenings out of seven. It would have kept me happy, and I would not have had to leave the babies for more than fifteen hours a week of their waking lives; this seemed to me to be so nearly fair a bargain that I was in despair at the thought of losing it. I knew that I would never again have so adequate a chance of satisfying my conflicting responsibilities, for jobs like that are naturally rare and heavily oversupplied. My needs are common needs. I had been looking forward to it for months: the thought of those three evenings at work, in a large impersonal building where no cries could reach me had kept me going through the exhausting business of pregnancy, birth, and sleepless nights. Joseph was a frightful baby: I did not sleep one night through until he was fifteen months old. Even David had been glad for my sake about the job, and had managed to contain his indignation at the way it had been got. He really hates Bob, the man who arranged it for me. Bob is a big fat, wealthy dilettante, who sees himself for some reason as my patron, and me in consequence as a saleable commodity; I like him, and am grateful for his interest, but David thinks he is the lowest of the low. He hates anything devious and well connected with almost suspicious passion. Whenever I am with the two of them, or talking about one to the other, I always find myself in the embarrassing position of liking in one man what I love the other man for condemning. Once, in the very early days of our acquaintance, David threw one of Bob's cameras through a pub window because he objected to Bob's taking photographs of a seedy old drunkard. But in this instance, with reference to this job, even he admitted that Bob had been of use.

I was thinking of this and watching the tele-

vision at the same time, trying to warn myself
about the loss that I had already accepted,
when David returned. I had been expecting
him to come back. I used to think he had real
rage in him, but after a year or two I found
that he did not rage, he sulked. Although enjoyment might keep him out all night, hunger,
annoyance or misery always drove him home.
He came in now, his head down and his hands
in his jacket pockets, that sombre, jutting look
on his features: a look I had seen so often,
on the screen, in publicity photographs, and
across the breakfast table, a look that used to
fill me with delightful terror, to make my knees
weak and the hair bristle on my scalp, and
that now merely wearily braced me to hours of
saddened combat. He sat down on the Chester-
field without taking off his jacket: it was a cold
night. I did not speak, though I looked at him
and nodded my head as a concession to his
appearance. I was not going to be the one to
speak first; I hoped that he might be overcome
with penitence, and that he would immediately
recant his sentence on the next year of my life.

We sat there for two minutes or so in silence:
I had reverted my gaze to the television and to
my book, and he was staring gloomily at the
carpet. As he continued not to speak, I wondered if he was noticing the patch where Flora
had spilled her cocoa earlier in the day; I did
not think so, it was I that noticed such things.
And when he did finally break our quiet inter-
locking, I realized that the carpet was far from
his thoughts, as indeed was the subject that he
broached.

"What are we going to have for supper then?" he said.

"Whatever you like," I said.

"Does that mean you haven't got anything?" he said, and without waiting for a reply he went on: "And for God's sake, switch the fire on, it's freezing in here. Why you have to sit in the cold all night I can't imagine."

I bent down and switched on the electric fire. "I'm used to the cold," I said smugly, to annoy. I am always vaunting over everyone, particularly over Dave, with his rugged pretensions, my capacity for endurance. I then continued, "You can have what you like for supper, eggs and bacon, chops, spaghetti, sausages. You can have whatever you want. Just tell me what you want and I'll go and do it."

"I know you don't want to go," he said. "You're watching that programme, aren't you?"

"Not really," I said. "Only because it happens to be on. Just tell me what you want and I'll go and cook it for you."

He wasn't going to be put in the wrong that way either.

"I'll get supper," he said. "Tell me what you want and I'll go get it."

"I don't want you to get my supper," I said, feeling my temper rising, knowing that he had caught me, as by that same stratagem he always did. "I'll get yours. If only you'd tell me what you want."

"You tell me what you want."

"I don't want anything. Shall I do you the chops?"

"I don't want chops."

"What do you want then?"

"You tell me what you want and I'll go and cook it."

And so we continued, in cold and weary rage, until I made my way to the kitchen to cook the chops, for that was the only way I could maintain an arguing position about that other, more profound affair; to add to my position, to creep another half inch higher up that muddy hill of domination, I actually peeled and boiled a pound of potatoes. So David got his supper, and I, let me face it, got mine, too, and a certain amount of credit as well.

We ate our supper in silence: I went on reading my book. Then, after watching a play on the television, I said that I was going to bed. I was very tired those days, owing to the smallness and voracity of Joseph, who was only seven weeks old. This assertion drove David into speech.

"Really, Emma," he said, "there's no need to be so furious about going to Hereford. What are you so annoyed with me about? Why don't you want to go?"

"I'm not at all furious," I said, loudly closing my book.

"Oh yes you are. What is it that you're so keen not to miss?"

"You know quite well," I said, "how much I was looking forward to this job."

"You can get another job. Someone like you can get any number of jobs."

"In Hereford?"

"Well, I'm sure there's something you could find to do there."

"You think so? Perhaps I could apply to be an usherette at your theatre, you mean?"

"Don't be ridiculous, my love. There must be something you can do."

"I'm sure, on the contrary," I said, "that there would be simply, literally nothing that I could do."

"You could look after the children."

"David my darling," I said, and I could still frighten him a little, though he could rarely frighten me, "don't you talk to me about those children. You have hardly any right to talk to me about those children. So kindly don't. Those children will be seen to all right, and it will be me that sees to them, so don't you bring them into any of our discussions."

"I can't think," he said after a pause, which signified defeat along that line, "why you wanted to do that job in the first place. A bloody silly way of spending your time, if you ask me. Just your vanity, I suppose; it's not enough for me to tell you that you're beautiful, you want the whole bloody nation to stare at you every night. Your vanity will kill you one of these days, you'll drop dead from selfishness if you don't watch it."

It was a better line, but I had my defences.

"What about you then?" I said. "I suppose you think acting is an art, don't you? It isn't even an art, it's just entertainment at its highest and prostitution at its lowest. And don't tell me that you're in it for the sake of the public, or any of that rubbish, you're in it for yourself, like all the rest of them, a pack of megalomaniacs, that's all you are. All you want to do is get your face in front of the public and yell, 'Get me get me get me.' That's all it is. Well, that's all right for you, get on with it, I don't complain about that. But let me have my bit, eh, let me get on with my little bit. At least I was going to tell the nation a lot of useful facts, politics and road accidents and trade union strikes. You get on with your sloppy emotional self-indulgence, pour your lovely self at the world, I don't complain."

"You're not in a position to complain," he said. "It's my lovely self that paid for those chops and that television and that dress you're wearing and that roof over your head."

"Ah well," said I, getting to my feet, "perhaps that's why I'm so keen on getting myself an independent income, so I can throw all this rubbish back in your charming face."

And I left the room. I went upstairs to bed; as I undressed I wondered if I was going to cry, but I didn't. I do not cry, and I was not really as cross as I thought I should be. I felt sorry for David: clearly he did want to go, and I don't think that it amused him to quarrel any more than it amused me. I read my book and tried to calm down; when he came upstairs again he was calmer, too. "Let's talk about it tomorrow," he said. "I haven't really signed the contract, you know. I wouldn't do a thing like that without telling you."

"I thought you wouldn't," I said.

He undressed and got into bed.

"I'm going to sleep," I said. "I'll just get a couple of hours before Joe wakes up again."

I arranged myself as for sleep; David laid one hand across my thigh. I twitched and pushed it off. He put it back on again. I pushed it off once more; he protested, I protested, he lost his temper. I lost my temper, and we started to quarrel again. That was how it was with us. David started off about living in the country: how charming it would be, greenery, cows, silences, and I retaliated about boredom. London means everything to me, noise and human beauty, I am not a one for the inhuman, and the thought of nature and the limited range of social patterns that would be presented for my inspection began to fill me with as much horror as the idea of losing my job had done. I would be lost out there with the cattle and the actors, lost and nothing.

"Hereford is probably so ugly," I said as I lay there between the sheets stiff with fright at the thought of it. "There won't be a single building except the cathedral; what will I look at for nine months of my life? We'll have to live in some foul semi-detached house, or some unspeakable flat. I can't bear it, I just can't bear it."

"I can't see what's so bloody marvellous about this house," he said, "as far as beauty goes."

"Well then," I said, "if you can't see that, you must be stone blind." And so, once more, we continued, for an hour and a half at least: in the end David got really angry, and at one of my more extreme insults to his profession he leaped up and beat his fist on the wall. Our house is an old house, an old Islington house, and his fist went right through the lath and plaster into nothingness, into the hollow middle of the wall itself. We both gave a yell of surprise; I reached out and switched on the light, and we stared at that gaping mouth, crunched so easily there into our wall, through

the William Morris wallpaper, the pride of my
life. As we watched a split appeared, reaching
right up to the picture frame, and bits of plaster began to fall thick on our heads like hail
from the decorated border of the ceiling.

"David," I said in an awed whisper when all
that would fall seemed to have fallen, "what on
earth have you done? And the best piece of
wallpaper in the house."

"How amazing," he said. "I hardly touched
it."

We were both awestruck; I was so impressed
that I was not even angry, for this seemed to be
a manifestation of the David I had known, the
man at whose approach graves opened, fountains leaped out of rocks, and trees and women
gathered to listen.

"Do you think the ceiling will fall in on us?"
I asked. Our anger had disappeared entirely:
we were holding hands, joined in admiration
for this extraordinary feat.

"Perhaps we ought to move the bed," he said.

So we got out and pushed the bed to another
part of the room; the noise of it woke Flora,
who had to be pacified, and Joe, who had to be
fed. By the time I had got Joe off to sleep again,
David and I were in a very gay mood and I
had consented to go and look at Hereford, to
read his script and to believe in his necessi-
ties. He in turn had consented to be understanding about having his hand pushed off my
thighs, in view of Joseph and my weariness.

When I finally got back into bed and arranged myself once more, I found that the
sheets were full of plaster; I lay awake some
time, feeling these small and gritty particles

rubbing against my legs. I thought of the princess and the pea, and that old myth about the sensitive skins of the world's aristocrats. I was certainly one of those, to judge by the irritation that those lumps of ceiling caused me. David, on the other hand, slept. Our marriage bed, pushed out into the middle of the room, stranded there far from the harbour of the walls and filled with grit, with David and myself far from unhappy in it. That perhaps was the beginning of the Garrick year, for me.

2

I SUPPOSE that some people may find it surprising that at this point we did not separate. Things being as they were, and I have tried to indicate how they were, why did I not stay in London at our house in Islington, which meant so much to me, and let David go off to Hereford by himself?

The reasons, some sordid and some not so sordid, are so clear to me that I can hardly forbear to tabulate them in sections and subsections. Amongst the sordid lay my fear of being left alone with the children and the nanny; my fear of public defeat; my fear of loneliness; my fear of the compensations for loneliness. And amongst the not so sordid lay each of these reasons, but seen in a milder and forgiving light. I did not want to separate the children from their father; I did not want anyone to criticize David for leaving me; I did not want David to be alone in Hereford, not only because I knew that if he went without me he would never come back, but also because I knew that he, too, would be lonely.

And yet despite the sections and subsections, the anatomy of our marriage, there remained something that could not be directed, for it was still alive; and it was this live thing that made it impossible for us to part. Indeed, the idea of parting never crossed our minds. It was never anything but a question of his staying or my going. This living thing, whatever it was, kept us still intertwined, so that at each move I knocked against him, each breath of his swelled against my own ribcage. We were not separate at this point: we were part of the same thing still. I like things to be orderly and distinct, I do not much like the mess of union, it made me angry that his ash should be in my ashtrays, that his movements should be my movements; and yet that was how it was. He said that he would go to Hereford, and I, self-willed, distinct, determined Emma Evans, I said that I would go, too.

When I think of that name he gave me, Emma Evans, I realize that I should have seen far earlier what a mess it was all going to turn out: a ludicrous name, a comic name, for a woman whose trademark had always been a certain bleak distance from such suggestions. I should have realized earlier. For someone of my intelligence, I have a good deal of ignorance to atone for.

I met David Evans four years ago in the Television Centre at White City. He was twenty-five at the time; I was twenty-two. We met by accident, in a lift, going up to the fifth floor. I was going to visit a friend of mine, with whom I was having lunch—the same friend Bob who later got me this other job which I had to turn down, though that was on another channel. I don't know where he was going. We did not speak, naturally, but we stared at each other and I wondered if I had seen him somewhere before. It was not a decisive meeting.

Our second meeting, however, was decisive. This took place on the last train from Charing Cross to Tonbridge, a few days after our preliminary encounter, and after I had seen him in the play on which he had clearly been working at the time when he had got into that lift. We were both in the same compartment; it was one of those sealed suburban compartments, with no corridor. I had got in first; he, walking along the platform and seeing me, had got in because I was there. I am glad of that: I believe in the significance of chronology. We eyed each other as the train drew out. We had not reached London Bridge before David said in his pronounced Welsh voice, which he uses to be charming, "Haven't we met somewhere before?"

"Yes, we have," I said. "We met in a lift at the Television Centre last week."

"Oh, really? Is that all? I had an impression that I knew you. . . ."

I did not reply to that: I was watching him

closely. He was wearing a jacket that he still
has, a navy blue, short, lumpy jacket. He
looked like an actor, he had all the air of self-
projection, of slightly extra physical delineation
that I associate with actors. Even the stubby
roughness of him was not mere roughness: it
was roughness that amounted in itself to gloss.

"Are you an actress?" was his next question.
"I'm sure I have seen your face somewhere before. Before that lift, I mean."

"Certainly I am not an actress," I said,
"though I'm quite well aware that you're an
actor, if that's what you mean."

"Oh?" he said. "What do you mean by that?"

"Well," I said, "I assumed that your curiosity
about myself amounted to nothing more than
a stimulation to my curiosity about you. That
you were giving me a lead-in, as it were."

He took that very well. We could always
make each other run.

"You're wrong about that," he said, "but
since you've broached the subject, I gather that
you do know who I am."

"Certainly I know who you are. I saw you
last Sunday night. David Evans, I believe."

"Now," he said, "you will have to tell me
how good you thought I was. If you do, I'll give
you a cigarette."

And he produced a packet from his pocket.

"I don't smoke tipped," I said, inspecting his
bargain.

"Don't you? I thought you would. I've got
some Gauloises somewhere." He hunted around
in his pocket and offered me a crumpled-look-
ing packet with only two left. Just as I reached

out my hand to take one he withdrew it and said:

"No, no, you haven't told me how good I was yet, you can't have one till you do."

"How do you know I saw the whole programme? How do you know I didn't switch off after the first ten minutes? How do you know I wasn't doing something else far more important at the same time?"

"Such as what?"

"There are a lot of things that one can do with the television on."

"All right then," he said, putting the packet away. "No flattery, no cigarettes."

We stared at each other, both a little grimly smiling, having established in a few quick minutes the very essence of provocation and bargaining for domination that was to characterize our curious conjunction. We are so alike that it alarms me.

I could see, after a while, that he intended to hold out on me, and the thought of that cigarette grew therefore increasingly attractive. He could no longer look me in the eyes: he had dropped his gaze, forfeiting as little as possible, to my knees, which were as usual exposed. It was thus that we passed through London Bridge. As we moved off again into the night, I said:

"All right then, I did think you were good. I didn't think you were bad, at any rate. I thought it was a rotten play, and I detest that girl, but I thought that you were quite good. You were the best thing in it, not that that is saying much. May I have my cigarette now, please?"

He got out his packet once more and handed me the cigarette. I was getting out a box of matches when he offered me a light. He held it so that I had to lean out to reach it: our knees met in the middle of the compartment, and he saw to it that our hands met, too. I could feel deep contractions of fright inside me.

We talked, for the rest of the journey, about this and that. We ascertained that I was getting off at the station before he was, though neither of us disclosed the cause of our journeys into unexpected Kent. He let me have the other Gauloise and smoked the tipped cigarettes himself. He said he did not like them; I asked him why he carried them around with him, and he said that he had got them for the woman he had taken out for the evening. As my station drew nearer and nearer and he still did not know my name or who I was or anything about me, I began to feel sick: waves of terror kept pouring through me. I shut my eyes and leaned back in the corner, with my hands folded on my lap. Through the cloth of my coat and skirt I could feel my guts heaving up and down. I said nothing.

"You've gone very quiet," David said as we drew in to my station.

"I'm very tired," I said as the train slowly, ominously ground itself to a halt. When it stopped, I died a small death; I could bear anything while that throbbing, rocking noise was going on, but the silence and the lack of movement were the end of me. Quite finished off, I opened the carriage door; he made no effort to help me, he was not that kind of person.

"Good-bye then," I said in those most cold

and distant polished tones of mine, those tones
of a *speakerine manquée,* and I got out. I
slammed the heavy door behind me and
turned away, and started to walk towards the
exit. I was already handing in my ticket when
he overtook me. He caught hold of my elbow
from behind: it seemed the kind of thing that
had happened to me a dozen times before, as
indeed in minor ways it had, but this was the
apotheosis of all such occasions, this was the
event itself.

"What on earth do you think you're doing?"
I said, shaking him off for the sake of human
dignity.

"I just thought I'd try it and see," David said,
handing in his ticket to the collector. The collector told him that he had got off at the wrong
stop, to which David replied with some rude
rejoinder, which would have annoyed me had
I been in a state of annoyance. Then we pointlessly wandered out together, into the shabby
car park in front of the station; we ended up
leaning against a railing under a street lamp.
The next thing I said was:

"That's the last train to Tonbridge tonight,
you know."

"I can walk," said David.

We stood there, under that lamp, not looking at each other, for a long time. Those minutes, however long they were, were the most
extraordinary of my life: I cannot think back
to them without writhing with some emotion,
nostalgia perhaps, or pride that I went through
them, or despair at the consequences of such
terror and such expectation. I myself, the surface of me, felt calm and dead and white in

that unnatural glare, and the part of me that
was not me, but just any old thing, the inside
of me, the blood and muscle and water and
skin and bone of me, the rubbish, was blazing
away, shuddering like some augur's sacrifice. I
have never been so frightened in my life, and
perhaps the whole of my effort since has been
nothing but a struggle to repeat that fright.

"I never asked you your name," he said.

"You could have asked me on the train."

"I could. But I didn't."

"You haven't got any more cigarettes to give
me for telling you."

"I'll buy you a hundred then, in the morning."

That was the kind of thing that I liked to
hear, and I said straight out, "My name is Emma Lawrence."

"Emma," he said with that Welsh double
consonant, and as he spoke the light above
went out. It must, I suppose have been midnight, or whatever hour they choose to extin-
guish the street lamps in that urban district.
In any case, it had the strangest effect, that
sudden darkness, as of sinking together into
some great depth. We moved together: I think
that we only took each other's hands, though
I have a memory of some more shocking union.

And that was it. He did walk back to Tonbridge that night, or so he has always asserted,
though his stamina has never been as remarkable as his capacity for rash assertions. Whatever he did, we parted after five minutes, with
addresses, telephone numbers and names carefully inscribed. I said that I had to go home,
which was not strictly true, but I was, as I had

also said, expected. And for a long time that
was all I knew about him, his address, his telephone number and his name. I was not interested in the rest. When he tried to tell me
about himself, I would stop listening: I did not
want to know. All I wanted was this feeling of
terror with which he inspired me. With him, I
felt that I was on the verge of some unknown
and frightful land, black desert, white sand,
huge rocky landscapes, great jungles of ferns.
Indeed, such personal attributes as I against
my will discovered in him I rather disliked: he
seemed in himself to be a stock character,
Welsh, pugnacious, dark, small, in childhood
religion-ridden and now ostentatiously keen on
drink and women, and with all this an actor, a
selfish, drama-besotted actor. In cold blood, in
bed alone or drinking my morning coffee, I
was stunned by the unlikelihood of it: my rare-
fied, connoisseur's self and this self-evident
cliché of a man?

We had an entrancing courtship, or affair,
rather, which was what we intended it to be.
We went to look at the gorillas in the zoo, a
fashionable pastime in those days for intellec-
tuals. We went to Highgate Cemetery, the
loveliest place in London, and kissed amongst
the tombs and dying wreaths while I mistaken-
ly tried to explain to him the reasons for the
charm of our surroundings. We went to Batter-
sea Park. We lay around in his room in Chel-
sea. And then, one day, we decided to get
married. I cannot now quite credit the casual
way that we arrived at this decision, and once
more I have to refer in my own mind to chronology, in order to make sure that we did not

marry because of Flora. We did not: that is a
fact. I think I married David because it seemed
to be the most frightful, unlikely thing I could
possibly do. I could not imagine what life with
him would be like. I imagined that it might be
a nightmare, an adventure, but whatever else
exciting: I thought that at the least he would
go at life hard, with his head down and his fists
clenched, forever. I did not want an easy life,
I wanted something precipitous, and with David I felt assured at least of that.

Nobody believed us when we said we were
getting married. And how right they were in
their scepticism. In the end they all assumed
that I must be pregnant, and started to offer
me varying kinds of advice, of which the best
came from my own father. Better an illegiti-
mate grandchild, he said to me after his first
meeting with David, than an ill-advised marriage. I told him that he was mistaken in his
premises, and he did not say any more. He is a
remarkably self-effacing man, and does not like
to browbeat anyone. David's parents were fortunately in too great a state of permanent
shock about David to bat an eyelid at the idea
of me: in fact, they only met me at the wedding ceremony, which took place in Cambridge, my father's home town. My father is a
theologian. The Evans parents were at first impressed by this, but they soon came to realize
how little it meant in any practical terms. They
were surprised that my father had managed to
reconcile alcohol and God, and were very bit-
ter about the champagne: I myself had to bring
up the marriage at Cana when nobody else
thought of it. At the end of the reception, ap-

parently, they were more outraged by my father than by anything else that they had seen. For a man who pretends to have faith, they said to my aunt, not knowing she was my aunt, he has remarkably little respect for the decencies of life.

After our marriage David and I got ground down. Until this time we had both deliberately kept each other at a breathless distance, with an instinct for sexual self-preservation of which we were not wholly aware. Once we were married, distance was no longer possible. Our passion for each other had been rooted, at the beginning, in our foreignness: in him, his flashy, commercial, charming, drunken, photogenic selfishness, and in me, my cool, professional, aesthetic, privileged, photogenic eccentricity. And in bed and at breakfast selfishness is not charming and eccentricity is not even eccentric. It is a common story, I know. Passion choked by domesticity. Or one might say that we married in haste and repented in leisure. Certainly we both were a catalogue of the vices in wife and husband that should act as a permanent deterrent from matrimony. And yet even in that worst patch I never managed to be sorry that we did it: it was a good gamble we made, each thinking that the other possessed the wildness to which we wished to chain ourselves forever, each thinking that we would by that one ceremony strap ourselves to the dusty wheels of the other's headlong career, each thinking that we had committed ourselves to unfamiliarity, so that we would be forever voluntarily exiled, with no pernicious hope of retreat, from that lush Cambridge garden and that sour four-room cottage in North Wales.

And we did achieve an exile, of course. We could hardly have achieved less. But in gaining so much for ourselves I sometimes felt that we had lost each other. It was not foreignness that began to weigh on my spirits, but familiarity. The details of our life together repelled me: I hated the way David would throw his clothes all over my neatly folded garments when he undressed for bed. I loathed the way that the bed itself would be strewn all over the room in the morning. When I sleep alone, I hardly disturb the sheets. And I know that my way of life infuriated him, too: he could never understand why it was necessary for me to take so long to do my hair, trying out new arrangements for an hour or more before I would go out for the evening, and after a few months he was no longer amused by my habit of wearing eccentric articles picked up in jumble sales and by my desire to fill the house with what he called Victorian junk.

After thirteen months we had Flora. I was furious: she was David's responsibility, we owed her to his carelessness, I was appalled by the filthy mess of pregnancy and birth, and for the last two months before she was born I could hardly speak to him for misery. But somehow, after she was born, and this again is a common story, I am proud of its commonness, things improved out of all recognition. We changed. I can see now that it is as simple as that: we changed. I was devoted to Flora, entirely against my expectations, so that every time I saw her I was filled with delighted and amazed relief. What I had dreaded as the blight of my life turned out to be one of its greatest joys. David, too, reacted overwhelmingly strongly towards the child, and in the shock of our mutual surprise at this state of affairs we fell once more into each other's arms. And so, for the next three years, we drifted on, in a quibbling, satisfactory kind of way, with a fairly normal distribution of happiness and woe; the only thing that never returned was my first rocky terror. The remarkable fact is that we were entirely faithful to each other. I do not understand why David was faithful to me: he says that he cannot count the girls that he had slept with before our marriage, and I believe him, though I am not as impressed by such statements as I used to be. So the reasons why he did not compensate for my periodic extreme unpleasantness remain hidden. The reason why I did not was, to me, quite clear: I never had time, and I never met anyone I liked. As simple as that. Even at the worst, I liked David. And although I did not see that I owed him very much, I certainly did not owe anyone else more.

And that is how things were before we went to Hereford.

3

ONE day in February, shortly after the discussion which caused David to push his fist
through the bedroom wall, he took me to Hereford to have a look round. It was a wise move
as it turned out. He hired a car for the day: we
did not have a car of our own. We could afford
to hire cars all over the place at a price which
bore no relation to value, but we could never
afford to buy one: our affluence, like that of
many actors, went hand in hand with a disastrous lack of capital. This hired car was nice
and spruce, its red plastic seats nattily fitted
over with transparent plastic loose covers, and
its heater was very effective, so I sat there warm
and benevolent, smiling at the passing countryside. It was a sunny cold day, and Joe was
asleep on my knee. We had left Flora behind:
she suffers terribly from carsickness. I am
afraid that she is a very high-strung child.

I had been reading, the night before, about
Garrick. It seemed that he had been born in
Hereford, as had Kemble, Mrs. Siddons and
Nell Gwynne, though of the four Garrick
seemed to me to be the most interesting character. As he had seemed, apparently, to whoever was responsible for naming the new the-

atre, which was to be the Garrick Theatre. The
old theatre, now long disused, had been the
Kemble. I liked the idea of Garrick: he seemed
to have been a happy man. And I liked what
Samuel Johnson said about him. "Sir," he said
to Boswell or some other when the other complained of Garrick's exuberance, "a man who
has the nation to admire him every night may
well expect to be somewhat elated." And when
he died, Johnson said that the gaiety of nations
had been eclipsed. Fine phrases, and doubtless
deserved. I also read about Garrick's own festival, which he had held at Stratford, in honour
of Shakespeare's bicentenary, and which had
been a disaster: the Avon had flooded and
carried away the pavilions and the refresh-
ments and all but the festive crew themselves. I wondered if anything as entertaingly
disastrous would happen to Wyndham Farrar's
effort this year.

My first sight of Hereford was enchanting. It
was late afternoon. It had taken us a long time
to get there: I had not realized how far west
we were going. David drove us straight to
Broad Street, and there, outside the cathedral,
he stopped the car. Joe woke at the cessation
of motion, but I ignored his wails, staring en-
tranced at these huge arches, pink in the dying
cloudy light. When I had looked at it for long
enough, we drove slowly back again along the
street, and I took in the gargoyles on the public
library, and the dark grey-green peeling defeated Corinthian pillars of the old Kemble
Theatre, and the smart iron colonnades of the
Green Dragon Hotel. I was enraptured: the
evening colour and the broadness of the street

itself had a holiday, foreign air, a charm not
of the everyday but of celebration.

Then we went to see the new theatre, which
was very close, just over the bridge on the other side of the river: it was too discreet for my
taste, I like nothing new that is not monstrous,
but its situation had a lovely watery elegance
which the architecture did not quite destroy.
David wanted to go in and have a look round,
but I thought that it would be too cold out for
the baby, so I let him go alone. I sat in the car
and waited, watching the water flowing endlessly under the bridge, and when he came
back I said:

"Well, all that we have to do now is to find a
house."

"You are ridiculous," David said, touching
my cheek with the hard knuckles of his hand.
"You only want to come because it looks pretty
today. If it had been raining, you would have
started all over again about London. Wouldn't
you?"

"Of course I would. You don't understand,
life is governed by accidents."

"Yours is. Mine isn't."

"That's what you think. What about the accident of meeting Wyndham Farrar at that
party? But for that the thought of you would
never have crossed his mind."

"Oh yes it would. Sooner or later. There's
nobody else for the parts."

"Megalomaniac." I bit his knuckle, which he
was still holding against me, in some defiant
gesture of his own towards contact.

"Seriously, Emma, will you be all right here?

You won't complain? Will you be able to find anything to amuse you?"

"I can tell you right now," I said as he started the engine, "that I shall complain. I shall come, and I shall complain. And I'll also tell you that if there's anything amusing to be found it will be me that will find it."

And so it was: although, of course, foreseeing those complaints and that amusement was so much more peaceful, so much more orderly and satisfying than undergoing them. This is always the case. Indeed, even in the case of our marriage perhaps the rocks and the speed and the dust that I had foreseen were exactly what I had found, though under one's tired feet the aspect of a distant landscape changes, and becomes endowed with human exhaustion, with blisters and sweat and broken nails.

The first objective, once my consent had been thus arbitrarily obtained, was to find ourselves a suitable house to live in. Rehearsals were to begin at the end of March; the season opened in May. I took charge of the house situation myself: David was inefficient about such things, and would have lived anywhere, provided that it was up to his opinion of his professional status, whereas I cared. Unduly, excessively, I cared. I had never lived anywhere that was less than beautiful: I had been brought up in Cambridge, in one of those large and lovely houses on Madingley Road, with shutters and an overflowing garden, and dark brick covered with plants and flowers. I had been sent away to an expensive and cranky girls' school, situated in a country house with yellow stone and garden statues. After that I had spent a year in Rome, in an apartment just behind the Piazza Navona, and from my bedroom at night I could see the fountains floodlit and that ancient arena. I had then lived for two years in a flat on Primrose Hill, which, though not of the classical and aristocratic grandeur to which I was accustomed, had a visual cachet of its own. When David and I got so aimlessly married, we had to find somewhere to live; we wanted to buy a house, to affirm, I suppose, in solid bricks and mortar the absurd nature of what we had done. I made myself unbelievably unpleasant about the purchase of it. I refused to look at anything in SW or NW as being too obvious a choice, and we could not afford plain W. I dragged David round the North and the South East, which he had never set foot in, trying to find the answer. I had no right to do this: the deposit was mine, but the mortgage was to be paid off by him. On the other hand, he did not care, and I did. So I trudged all over London, and I enjoyed it: I felt as I walked that I was learning something, even if it was only the names of the streets. I wrote to every estate agent in the professional directory, and every morning our doormat was thick with envelopes and brochures. I would lie in bed for hours reading them, then get up and spend the day in search. I was obsessed. David said I was mad, and perhaps he was right.

The house that I found was the right thing. As soon as I saw it, it fitted neatly into some ready-made notch: it was an ordinary nineteenth-century terrace house in Islington, and on either side of the front door stood a small stone lion. Inside it had been modernized by a young couple who had since made a lot of money and moved off into a more fashionable area. It was all right: nothing remarkable, except for the plaster ceilings and one good ornate fireplace. But the back garden was up to the standard of the lions. It was surrounded by a high brick wall, but from the upstairs rooms one could see it and all the gardens in the row, and the impression was of old brick and shoots of greenery and grass and daffodils. Our garden was all weeds, but the one next door on the right had been looked after to perfection by an old man who had lived in the house through all the permutations of the area, from its days of respectable solidarity, the days in which Dickens refers to "shady Pentonville," through the shabby slip into dusty urban poverty and back once more into the classless rise of chi-chi that David and myself quite adequately represented. His garden was a perpetual delight: the grass was mown and even, flowers grew at every season in every corner and the walls were covered with every variety of climbing, blossoming plant.

In the street in front of the houses there was nothing but dust and hard brick and cars and dirty children. One would never have guessed what secret foliage grew behind that stony frontage.

I know that my attachment to such things and the importance that they assume for me verge in the eyes of others on the irresponsible. I am not happy that the opinion of such people should be bad, but I am made how I am made. Throughout my life I have been accused of

snobbery, in some form or another, and I do not
like it, I wish it were not so. I have no desire
to exclude; on the contrary, I would rather in-
clude, I would rather at every moment recognize, and am I to blame that the occasions on
which I can do so are so rare? I suppose that
I am to blame. I carry a great weight of blame
around with me, the price of my distinctions;
but I will go on carrying it, for to cease to
distinguish is an impossibility, and I will traffic only in possibilities and facts.

I set about Hereford as I had set about London: I wrote to the estate agents, I advertised
in the local papers, I rang up the theatre management. It was impossible, negotiating over
all that distance, and I could not keep going up
and down to inspect things personally because
of Flora and Joe's feeds and the transport. In
the end, when there was less than a fortnight
to go before our removal, I accepted an offer
of an ancient house in a long, low terrace of
ancient houses, in the old part of the town. It
was small, and the ground floor had been a sta-
ble and was now a garage. The only real alternative had been a modern and doubtless extremely ugly detached residence, in a row of
other such residences, in an expensive quiet
road. I knew that the house I had accepted
would probably be falling to pieces, but I
thought that I was prepared to put up with
any discomfort for the sake of the possibility of
a little dignity. Also, I like houses built not
alone but as blocks. I like terraces and apart-
ments.

You may ask, did I ask David's opinion? No,
I did not. He would have opted every time for

the central heating and the small square garden. And how very right he would have been,
in every way except the way in which I make
my rigorous decisions.

And so, after the wonderful task of packing
and despatching our clothes, our crockery, a
carefully selected array of old china, embroidered screens, stone heads and so forth, all
lovingly packed by me, with such pride in my
own skill and efficiency, we finally arrived at
Paddington Station just before midday, David
and I, encumbered only by one small suitcase,
our French girl, Pascal, Flora and a large plastic boat, and Joe in a carrying cot. We had
arrived half an hour early, naturally, and had a
reserved compartment. We put Pascal and Joe
into the compartment, then David, Flora and I
set off to have a look around the station. I must
confess that I was quite excited: I like journeys, I like stations; it is not that I am full of
hope, but I am easily filled with some kind of
anticipation which could well be mistaken for
it.

Flora, too, was very excited. She was walking
between us, holding a hand each, very soberly;
she was wearing, I remember, her red trousers
and her brown corduroy coat. I am proud of
her, in a painful way. We looked at the war
memorial, and the shiny plaques on the plat-
forms bearing the coats of arms of all the West-
ern countries. David showed me that of the
County of Wales, where he had been born and
reared. I had never been there.

"I'll take you," he said. "Sometime during
the season I'll take you to Wales." We smiled
at each other, over Flora's small dark head:

like children, we were both of us easily cheered or bribed by the promise of an excursion.

Then we went to the chemist's to buy a packet of cleansing tissues, which I did not really need, but I always feel that I should avail myself of the facilities of public places. On the way back to our platform we passed a poster for the Hereford Festival; it was a well-designed piece of work. Wyndham Farrar, it said in very large letters, and in almost · as large letters the names of his artists: Natalie Winter, Peter Yates, Felicity White, David Evans, Neville Grierson, all with prominent billing. We stood and stared at it. David was delighted, though as ever too suspicious of me to reveal it. There was a list of the plays there, too, about which I knew little: *The Clandestine Marriage*, *The White Devil*, *The Maple Tree*. As we finally got on to the train, I asked David about them.

"What's *The White Devil* about?" I asked him as we settled down.

"I've no idea," he said. "I've never read it."

"That's nothing to be proud of."

"I'm not proud of it. I just haven't read it, that's all."

"What's your part about then?"

"It's the best part in the play."

"How do you know if you haven't read the thing?"

"I can tell from looking at it. It's the longest. And Wyndham said it was the best."

"Don't be so gullible, he obviously says that to everyone."

"Anyway, it's a very good part. It's Natalie Winter's brother."

"How nice for you. Nice or nasty?"

"Definitely nasty. A rotten bastard and a so-cial climber and a pimp."

"Very suitable," I said.

"And a very nice death scene."

"Really?"

"I die on stage."

"That should be very sweet and charming," I said, and Flora, who had been listening intently, said with sudden yearning, "Sweeties, sweeties," having in a truly significant fashion extracted from our altercation the one word which she thought might concern her. I did not want to start on the inevitable stickiness so early in the journey, but the sight of her earnest small face, prepared to express the greatest depth of tragic deprivation, made me hunt in my handbag for a tube of mints. I spoil the child, for I can never believe the passion she expresses about sweets, toys, the ducks in the park or a dropped and dirtied apple is as transient and shallow as it clearly must be. I take her too seriously, my daughter, as I take all others.

As the train started to move, I felt, despite my irritation with David and my succumbing to Flora, a sudden hopeful pleasure. I looked up at the soaring wooden arches and then we were gone. The movement of the train calmed me, that soft repetitive motion against which I could lie limp as a doll, all the erect rigidity with which I face the world jolted out of me, my attempts at rhythm taken over by those crude padded pistons. I watched Flora as we moved through the suburbs of London: she was perched on the edge of the seat, chewing her peppermint and looking at Peter Rabbit, as tense and rigid as she ever was. Nothing would still her now, not the train, nor a rocking chair, nor my arms, until she was at the last stage of exhaustion. Poor Flora, who was I to deny her peppermints?

Half an hour later we all went to have lunch. I tried to persuade Pascal to stay with Joe and let David and myself go, but Joe woke as we discussed it, so I carried him along with me and we all installed ourselves, with Joe on my knee and Flora sitting primly beside me. It would have been more convenient to pack a picnic meal, but picnic meals do not appeal to me, and I have always made a principle of suiting myself rather than the children. Whether this is efficiency or obstinacy I do not know, but it is a fact that Flora can already behave with perfect nonchalant neatness in hotels, tea shops and classy restaurants. We were just studying the menu when a man and a girl arrived and sat at the two-seater table on the other side of the gangway; the man noticed David, and hailed him avidly.

"Hello, hello, Dave," he said plummily and loudly. "Having lunch with the family, are you?"

"That's right," said Dave, staring round at the brood of women and tiny, hardly masculine Joe, four whole people with whom he had carelessly encumbered himself in the last four years. I could read it on his face, his amazement, and I did not much pity him for it.

"Emma," he said, "have you met Michael Fenwick? Michael, this is my wife, Emma. All the rest are children and foreigners."

Pascal, who continued after several months
to find David's rudeness appealing, smiled and
nodded. Flora continued to read the menu:
she did not think Michael Fenwick worth her
attention. And she was, basically, right. I had
in fact met him once before, at a party; he
was a middle-aged man, probably a little over
forty, and he had a quality of fleshy heavy
childishness that I found quite frightening. I
did not like him: the way he seemed perpetually to extend a sentimental, boneless arm, plead-
ing for approval, upset me. I like to feel that
my words or gestures are going to bounce
brightly, harmlessly back at me, but with a
man like Michael they sink into some warm,
vulnerable tissue, wounding, however harmless
in intention, as they go. He always plays on
stage big, heavy, strong men, and is not at all
bad at it; but, oh, the floppy frightful contrast
in the wings.

Michael was sitting with this girl, who
seemed at first glance to be far more worthy of
inspection. Michael introduced her, and her
name rang an immediate and reverberating
bell.

"This is Sophy Brent," he said, "Sophy, David and Emma Evans. David is playing in *The
Clandestine Marriage;* you knew that, didn't
you?"

"And you, of course, are playing Fanny,"
said David, staring at her with his usual offen-
sive flattery. And for once I did not blame
him: I could not take my eyes off her myself.
She was wearing a white head-square and a
pale grey mackintosh, unbuttoned over a delightful brown jersey. Under the head-square

her hair leaped strenuously upwards, thick, dark hair, too strong for the silk to flatten. She had a perfectly shaped face: huge brown eyes, long brown cheeks and very wide lips, painted in a dazzling shade of orange. A full, gentle, voracious, suggestive face, and for some reason an obviously stupid one. I cannot think why I was so certain at first sight of her relative stupidity: it surely cannot have been the old adage about beauty and brains, which I have seen disproved both ways often enough. And her clothes were extremely good. I do not remember that I have ever seen Sophy wear anything frightful, except for one patterned shirt which she wore once and then immediately abandoned. It may have been something in the lavishness of her appearance, in the high gloss on her and the undue brightness of her nails that gave me the warning; or perhaps she was merely the perfection of a type with which the theatre is filled, the girl who is in the theatre because she thinks her looks are too good to waste at home. Sophy dresses well, her accent and voice are all that they should be and yet somewhere underneath it all everyone can sense something wild and ripe that gives her away.

We talked, across the gangway, about the season, and Hereford, and how pretty we thought it would be in spring. They all talked very loudly, those three, so that the whole of the carriage could and did listen. I have never decided whether actors cannot help talking loudly or whether they think that the unpaying public actually enjoys the privilege of listening to them. A little of each, perhaps. I watched

Sophy, and Sophy watched David, and David watched Sophy. Michael watched everyone, and ordered a bottle of British Railways wine because he did so like everyone to be happy and cozy.

"What a lovely start to the season, meeting you like this," he said from time to time. I could tell that Sophy, in fact, got on his nerves, as I did. David was all right: for one thing, he was a man, and for another thing, he had a certain professional matiness which he did not mind using on Michael's behalf; but on the whole, as a gathering, we were a little too sharp and silly for his taste.

I noticed that Sophy was not bothering to watch me. I knew why: it was because I had a baby on my knee. You underestimate me, my girl, I said to myself; and when David had finished his dry and tepid chicken I handed Joe over, just to remind her of his paternity, while I attacked the remainder of my meal. David immediately handed him to Pascal, but I could see that the idea had sunk home. "What an adorable baby," she cried when Joe finally ended up on Pascal's knee, next to the gangway and next to her. "What's his name?"

"Joseph," I said.

"What an unusual name," said Sophy. "Do you call him Joe? And what's the little girl called?"

"Tell Sophy your name," I said to Flora, who stared back at me reproachfully, pausing in her task of eating, one by one, a plateful of peas. "Go on, tell her your name." Flora said nothing.

"Perhaps she's shy," said Sophy.

"Go on, tell her your name," said David.

"No," said Flora, and ate another pea.

"She's called Flora," I said. "She doesn't really know what her name is yet. She isn't two yet."

"Do you mean," said Sophy, "that you've got two children both under the age of two?"

"That's right," I said. Michael Fenwick was looking disgusted, and I sympathized with him. Sophy looked appalled and pitying, and I could understand her feelings, too. And yet, for all that, they had both of them alienated themselves from our tableful by their reactions: those with children, however unwillingly with them, are in many ways irrevocably cut off from those without, and David and I watched Flora pursuing her peas with a unity of enthusiastic tenderness that we could not feel for anything else, and that they, those other single two, could feel for nothing. As we watched her, she dropped one on her knee.

"Oh, the pea!" she exclaimed in her tone of pure amazement, and started to hunt for it with her spoon. David and I smiled at each other, and he leaned over and retrieved it for her. She would not let him put it in her mouth, he had to put it on her plate so that she could pick it up again with her spoon. I recognize myself in her at every turn, my own obstinate artifact of life. And I said to myself, There must be more unlikely people than David and myself who have become fathers and mothers, harnessed to this domestic machinery, but I could not think of any.

On the way back to our compartment we passed Natalie Winter. She was sitting with a book on her knee, and happened to look up and smile as we passed. David opened the door and said, "Hi, Nat," and she said, "Hello, David, hello Emma," and then could not think of anything else to say, so we moved on. She was a very shy woman. She was also the star of the season, and was to play Vittoria in *The White Devil* and the lead in the new play, *The Maple Tree*. She would have been a perfect illustration of the belief (had it been true) that all actors and actresses are very ordinary, unglamorous people at heart. I had met her several times, mostly at dressy occasions, and every time she had looked quite dreadful, a governess dressed up in clothes she thought an actress should wear. I remember one dress, layer upon layer of pink frill, from which her bony neck and shoulders rose in vulnerable inelegance. In her railway compartment she was wearing a tweed coat, and looked more at home. Her hair was pale, wispy and short, and her face pale and tremulous. Nobody would look at her twice, and yet she is the genuine thing, and one of the few actresses that I admire, one might almost say a great, a classical actress. On stage she always looks enchanting. She is a doctor's daughter, and has never been known to say anything of interest to anyone.

Thinking of Natalie and Sophy Brent and Michael Fenwick, I sat down once more and watched the wet, grey-green countryside, where the beginnings of leaves hung on the bushes in their first painful prickings. And I, too, was full of buds and nervous colour, after my impersonal childbearing winter. There would be, in Hereford, a whole new society

waiting for me, and who could say what I
might not find, a friend, an enemy, a lover, or
that somebody like myself that I see once a
year in the back of a passing taxi or drawing
the curtains of an upstairs room? And how
nice, how nice all this open grassy land would
be for the children: what picnics, what sun-
bathing, what walks by the river we could
have.

When we arrived at Hereford, it was pouring
with rain. I did not think quickly enough as
we unpacked, with the result that the few
available taxis were filled with Natalie Winter,
Sophy Brent and various other characters before we had passed the ticket barrier. We had
to wait in the rain for one to return. I was
annoyed: I felt that David would think I
should have thought about this problem, although I knew at the same time that such a reflection would never cross his mind and that
waiting in the rain did not upset him in the
least. When we finally got off, I noticed that the
streets looked amazingly depressing. I told myself that this was simply the nature of all station approaches, but there was very little
improvement in the decor before we arrived at
our destination. The house itself did not look
too bad, and the street had a certain low-built,
peeling, historical look, but the wetness and
greyness were enough to damp any enthusiasm. I had so hoped it would be sunny.

But the exterior of the house was nothing on
the inside. The front door let one into a large
garage, where our packing cases were waiting
for us and a narrow uncarpeted staircase led
up to the first floor, which was the habitable

part of the dwelling. I did not mind that un-
conventional approach, though I did not like
the fact that the staircase was not boxed in
and the banisters looked far enough apart for
Flora to squeeze through if she tried, as she
inevitably would try. What lay at the top of
the stairs, however, was too grim for words. It
was not the bricks and mortar, it was the furniture.

In the living room, which was the first room I
looked at, there was a modern three-piece suite
with wooden arms, upholstered in a bright
shade of peacock blue. In my opinion, peacock
is a colour that suits peacocks and nothing else.
There was also, occupying the whole of one
wall, a large brown sideboard with curly wood-
en appendages: not carvings, just brown useless twists of nasty varnished wood. The carpet
was bright red with brown flowers, and looked
as though it were new. So, on inspection, did
the three-piece suite. Apart from two flower
vases with an iridescent finish, there was little
else in the room. Having taken this in, I moved
on, a little dazed, to the dining room, which
contained a shiny, apparently unused table of
such a strange, yellowy-white tint that I
thought at first it must be made of some kind of
synthetic material. It was surrounded by four
chairs with high curved backs and upholstered
red seats. There was also a tall yellow cupboard which looked as though it contained
crockery. I did not have the courage to open it.

I made myself go on and look at the bed-
rooms, knowing already what they would be
like. I could see all the time a vision of a conscientious landlord rubbing his hands with re-

lief and thinking how well he had acquitted himself. And he had, too: there was no possible cause for complaint. The prize piece in our bedroom, and indeed, about the only other piece apart from the bed, was a wardrobe, a round-ended, round-topped wardrobe, with a high and streaky gloss. It was so large that it almost blocked the entrance into the room. The frightful pointless utility of its shape and its surface overwhelmed me, and I sat down on the bed and slowly began to unbutton my coat. If I had been given to crying, I might well have cried. If I did cry, this is the sort of thing that I would cry for. After a while David followed me upstairs. I could hear Flora running about gaily in the barnlike garage below.

"What's the matter?" said David when he had opened the wardrobe door, shut it again and inspected himself in the mirror.

"Nothing's the matter."

"Which room is Pascal having? She wants that one with the yellow bedspread. She thinks it's lovely."

"She can have whatever she wants," I said.

"All the packing cases are in the garage," said David. "I think everything's arrived. Do you want to go and have a look?"

"I have no desire at all to go and have a look," I said.

"What is the matter, Emma? I think it's very nice, don't you?"

"No, I don't," I said. "I think it's unspeakably hideous. I just can't live in a place like this."

"I don't see what's wrong with it."

"Don't you?"

"I thought this was the kind of place you like."

"Oh, David."

"Well, you chose it."

"Yes, but I hadn't seen it. Anyway, it's not the house, it's the furniture."

"What's wrong with the furniture? It all looks jolly good stuff to me." And he gave the wardrobe an approving slap.

"David," I said, neatly folding up my headsquare into smaller and smaller triangles, "can't you see how frightfully ugly it is?"

"Ugly? Yes, I suppose it is quite ugly. But it'll do to hang clothes in, won't it? It's clean, isn't it?"

"I think it's new," I said, and he opened it again and looked inside. It smelled of sawdust.

"Yes, it's new," he said.

"Well then, whoever would buy an object like that? Whoever would buy one, with real money? You realize it probably cost four times as much as ours at home with the shells on? Think of somebody going into a shop and deliberately choosing a thing like that. Who could do it, what kind of person could do it?"

"Well, people like me, for example," said David, who had sat down at a dressing table and was admiring his reflection once more. "That's exactly the kind of thing I would probably buy if you left me to buy you your furniture. And you married me, didn't you?"

"I didn't marry you for your taste in furniture."

"What I meant was, there's no need to condemn whoever bought that just because they bought it. Bad taste isn't a crime, is it?"

"But, David, can't you see what it's like?"

"I suppose I can, now that you point it out."

"And it's totally valueless. That kind of thing has no value whatsoever. You couldn't resell it for five bob, not even the day after you bought it, although it must have cost fifty pounds."

"Why worry about that? The place'll look a lot different when you've unpacked our stuff. It just looks a bit bleak at the moment. It's not yours, you haven't got to do anything about it but live with it for a bit. People live in places much worse than this, you know. You should see the places I've stayed in when I've been in rep. This place is bloody marvellous, if you ask me."

"I can't live here," I said feebly.

"Don't be ridiculous, woman." He was watching, I could see, the mirrored image of his own reactions. "You'll just have to live here, that's all. You'll just have to learn to put up with what other people would give anything to have. I can tell you that there will be a lot of people here who'd give anything to be able to afford to live in a nice house like this for the season. You're spoiled, that's what's the matter with you."

"Well, if I am, that doesn't make it any the simpler, does it? I can't tell you what that wardrobe does to me. It depresses me."

"You just don't like anything that's less than a hundred years old. You should be dead and buried. That wardrobe, that's modern life. You'll just have to ram it down your gullet and swallow hard."

As usual, the more grandiose of his state-ments managed to silence me. For it was modern life, that wardrobe, and I knew as I stared at it that I was going to do my best to swallow it; but I protested, nevertheless.

"It's not modern life at all," I said. "It's just hideous hybrid nothingness."

"The only conclusion to draw then," said David, who is far from stupid, "is that we live in a hideous hybrid age, and I know you won't have that, will you? You swallow down your nasty sweet martini, you smoke your cigarettes, you watch the filthy television, you speak up in praise of posters and office blocks and speedboats and jazz, you spend a bleeding fortune on lacquer to keep your hair in ridiculous shapes and then your stomach won't accept an ordinary useful inoffensive wardrobe. You can't just have what you want and throw out the rest, you know."

"I suppose I'll get used to it," I said. "If it exists, it exists, and it might as well exist in my bedroom as anyone else's."

"That's the spirit," said David, leaving the mirror and coming over to sit by me on the bed. "I knew you'd see it that way. I don't see it that way myself, but I knew that you would."

"You think you can talk me round, do you?"

"Why not? I only say to you what I know you would be thinking in half an hour's time. I just try to hurry up the misery, that's all. Now give me a nice kiss."

"What for?"

"For being so understanding about that wardrobe. I'll tell you something: you did marry me for my taste in furniture after all, you know. You married me because my taste was so bloody awful, and you thought it would be good for you to be up against it every day of your life. Isn't that true?"

"Of course it's true."

"And I'll tell you something else: I, like that wardrobe, am modern life. In its less desirable aspects. How far down your gullet do you think I've got?"

"You've stuck," I said. "You've stuck."

"You mean I'm not digested?"

"Not at all digested. You're all raw and whole and hairy."

"Give me a kiss, Emma."

"I don't much feel like giving you a kiss. I don't feel like kissing anyone."

"I'll help you unpack if you give me a kiss."

"I don't want you to help me unpack, you'll break everything," I said, but nevertheless I slowly turned my face towards him and our lips met and rested together. And so we sat for a moment, as I thought, tasting his familiar tobacco flavour, that our lips might be there, but where, in the words of the song, were our hearts? There was more between us two than a wardrobe.

4

BY THE next morning I had managed to convert the house to something nearer the kind of

house I might live in. I did this by covering
all ledges and surfaces with my carefully ac-
cumulated objects and scraps of tattered and
embroidered cloth. I could see Pascal getting
sadder and sadder as the transformation took
place: she really hated my style, that pale shiny
table was just about her measure, and she cried
out in protest as it disappeared under a green
fringed velour cloth that had belonged to my
grandmother. What a strange situation the domestic situation is that it should oblige one to
live with other people with whom one has no
sense of connection of any kind. Pascal and I
disagreed, I am sure, on every possible point,
and yet we lived together, ate together, shared
the same bath and the same life. I was a little
surprised that she agreed to go to Hereford
with us at all. I suppose that it was her dotty
devotion to David that kept her with us. He
used to tease her, and hold her hand, and comment on her clothes: he had his uses. And
daily, nightly, Pascal and I would exchange
remarks, for months on end, and yet for all that
I knew about her she might have been a total
stranger. This, I am sure, was a direct result of
our relationship, of the economic nexus that
bound us. I knew more about someone that I
met for ten minutes at a party than I knew
after months about Pascal. Not that I ignored
her because I paid her; on the contrary, the
fact that I was paying her afflicted me so much
that I did not dare to intrude, by a look or a
word, upon her privacy. Perhaps she did not
care, but I cared. I treated her with such infinite respect that I did not criticize a single
one of her actions, nor go so far as to open her

bedroom door to see what she had done to the
room, for the whole of the time she was with
us. The result of all this circumspection was
that I did not know what she was like, and I
set great store by knowing what people are
like.

While I was unpacking I found that one of
my Liverpool ware teapots was broken. I had
two, both with delicate grey-and-white pastoral
scenes of cows and trees; and one of them,
as I unpacked, was already in pieces. I had
packed it too near the edge of the tea chest;
it must have been knocked in transit. It was my
own fault, and I had never broken anything
in removal before. I was white with fury for an
hour after. It is frightening how little I can
bear any slipping off of my own perfection.

That night, the night after our arrival, we
had been invited to a civic reception by the
town, to be held for the company. I think that
it was the thought of that which kept me so
tolerably gay throughout our settling in; it was
certainly not David, who disappeared as soon
as we had had breakfast on our first day there,
saying he was called for a rehearsal, which I
did not believe. He did not reappear all day.
So I dressed for this public event alone. I knew
that it was going to be entertaining. There is
nothing that I enjoy more than watching, from
some safe, anonymous position, such as that of
wife, the magnificent, sprawling, guerrilla war-
fare of such absurd human functions, and I
have found that where actors are concerned
the gaiety for the observer is doubled. I took a
great deal of trouble over my appearance, for
I, too, wished to look absurd. I wore a black

velvet suit, which is perfectly respectable by any standards, if a little smart, and under it a white blouse I had made myself, the front and cuffs of which were covered in tiny, thick starched lace frills. I was very proud of it: it had taken me weeks to make, and the result had a delightful archaic, Victorian photograph quality. As I put it on I decided that I would have to wean Joseph: my breasts were too big. They looked all right, but misrepresentative.

I spent hours trying to put my hair into earphones, but I succeeded in making myself look too hideous even for amusement, so I abandoned the attempt and put it all up on top. Then I got out an old black hat and a sequin bag that I had bought from the old lady who keeps a junk shop round the corner from us in Islington. I had paid half a crown for each, and was gratified to think that I had found a truly suitable occasion for using them. The hat was a very fine straw, with feathers and a black lace rose; the bag, which the old lady had told me used to be her dance bag, was of silver sequins, tarnished by now to a grey and black and ancient dignity. When I had finished, I thought I looked wonderful: they would have difficulty in knowing what to make of me, at least. I could not decide whether the final effect might not be funereal. Certainly I had a bizarre sobriety. I have no colour at all in my flesh, ever: I am dun- and mud-coloured, and you would not think to look at me that blood runs in my veins.

I was just wondering whether to leave for the reception alone when David returned from town, or from wherever else he had been. He walked into the bedroom and took a look at me.

"Emma," he said, "whatever have you done?"

"What do you mean?" I said coldly, anticipating his usual tasteless insults, but all he said was:

"You look wonderful, that's all."

"Aren't you going to change?" I said.

"Why the hell should I? For a lot of old ladies?"

"Who says they're going to be old ladies?"

"Well, won't they be?"

I knew he would not change, and I did not want him to: I like him best when he looks a mess. I like the effect we create together, he so aggressive, I so formal. Oddly enough, he was wearing a tie. He does, sometimes. On the way out I went to say good night to Flora, who was in her bath.

"Bye-bye, Mummy," she said, joining the two words together with careful effort. When I am puzzling about the location of my heart, I have only to look at Flora to discover what seems at times to be the whole of it. Though at other times it seems to be elsewhere. As we left, Pascal said:

"*Bonne soirée.*"

She looked stunned by the hat. The rest got by, but she could not take her eyes off my hat, though in the standards of absolute beauty the check-cloth caps that she had recently taken to wearing, obeying the dictates of the day, could not compete. The hat that I had on had weathered sixty years with grace, and that in itself was something. I should not complain if I myself could batter my way through to such a survival, my shape and my roses withstanding, though threadbare, the shifts of fashion.

The reception was all that I had hoped. When we arrived we were shown into some kind of anteroom, where we were detained, with the rest of the actors; apparently we were not yet allowed to mingle with the other guests, though what we were waiting for was far from clear. Pointlessly we eyed each other; David was getting annoyed, as he always does when drink is withheld, and would not introduce me to anyone. Nor would he speak to anyone, so he and I stood together crossly, waiting for something to happen. There seemed to be no point in discussing Flora's linguistics, or the gas water heater, which would never ignite, so we said nothing. I stared hard at people to stop them staring at me; this is one of my amusements. After about five minutes we were suddenly all ushered through into the main hall, where the town dignitaries were already drinking their sherry. I gathered that Wyndham Farrar and the Mayor were shortly to say a few words, so I hastily ditched David and tried to find myself a drink. I did not have much success until I located the kitchen door and stood by it till the next full tray issued forth, whereupon I immediately helped myself. Then I prepared to have a look round. As I had expected, all the actors were still gathered together in a tight huddle, and nobody was making any effort to perform introductions. It was like the school dances I used once to attend, at which all the boys stood along one wall and all the girls along the other. But here the division was social, not sexual.

A few of the better-known figures, such as
Natalie Winter, were eventually urged to cross
the gap by obsequious attention. She was wearing a cocktail dress in emerald green, a colour
better left to emeralds, with a black satin evening bag and white satin shoes. She did not
sort at all ill with the town ladies, some of
whom were attired in a very similar way; she
was talking to a middle-aged couple, with an
air of some embarrassment. David, also, I soon
noticed, had attracted the attention of a group
of women, who were chattering round him; he
looked quite at home. He had, of course, a better-known face than many of the better-known
actors in the company; there were many people
who had heard of Natalie Winter but never
seen her, but many more who had seen David
Evans though never heard of him. It was to
make himself heard of that he had joined the
company at all. He wished, for some reason, to
be a classical actor, did David.

I wandered round, exchanging a word or
two with actors I had met before. On my trav-
els I passed a woman six feet tall dressed in
bright orange, a small lady in a tweed suit
and a vast and flowery straw hat, and a man
who had spilled sherry all down his shirt front.
All the actors that nobody had ever heard of
were still clustered together, shy and defensive,
muttering anxiously to themselves. It amused
me to think of those two whole separate worlds
crowded into one room and not touching at
any point; I knew a little of each world, myself,
of the town with its doctors and farmers and
landowners and headmasters, and of the theatre, with its pretty young men and its neurotic

young women, and its bores and its stars, and
I had nothing to do with either of them. I had
nothing to do with anything, and yet I was
there. What could be happier than that?

Just before the Mayor embarked on his
speech, I noticed Sophy Brent. She was dressed
in black, as I was, and she was all shiny and
gay. She was talking to a group of pressmen,
who were taking her photograph from time to
time as she spoke. She was clearly in her ele-
ment: she was made, one could tell, for that
gluttonous negative machine.

The Mayor said most of the things that one
would have expected him to say: what a distinguished company, what a pleasure for the
town to have a live theatre again, and so on.
From his speech there emerged something that
I had not known, the kind of thing that David
would not think to remember to tell me: it
seemed that although the Arts Council had
done its usual small best, most of the money
for the enterprise had been provided by a
wealthy American lady who fancied herself
to be in some way related to Garrick. She had
apparently been an actress herself before the
marriage that had left her with this vast sum.
It was the kind of story that enchants me, it
seems so unlikely, and so often happens. The
theatre must, I think, be peculiarly prone to
romantic aberrations of this kind, for in it people are always discarding the checks of common sense and allowing the more ridiculous
elements in human nature to take over, the
elements of gross vanity, or jealousy, or even
generosity. I liked the idea of this Mrs. Von
Blerke, who was not in fact present, though

she was due to arrive in time for the opening
night. Her gift explained to me the seemingly
pointless gesture of building an expensive new
theatre in this particular spot, which could not
possibly, although small, be filled all the year
round. An empty theatre, dedicated to the vanity of human kinship. Though this year, or so
David assured me, it would be full: he thought
people would travel from the ends of England
to watch his performances, I think.

After the Mayor, Wyndham Farrar spoke. He
spoke slyly, or so it seemed to me, concealing
rather than revealing what he really had to say.
He spoke in general about the theatre in the
provinces, and about the National Theatre;
then he spoke about Mrs. Von Blerke and local
benefactors. He did not make a single original
remark, and he spoke for ten minutes. I was
disappointed. I do not know what I had been
expecting him to say. No enthusiasm could
have touched me, myself so unenthusiastic, so
had I absurdly been expecting some giveaway
sceptical stroke that would have matched my
own doubts? Certainly, even though he said
nothing to encourage me, I had a sense that his
own interests could not be either as philan-
thropic or as naïve as they appeared. His very
manner promised duplicity. Or perhaps it was
the myth of his greatness that had touched me:
I was unwilling to admit that this man, who
was, they said, different, could be exactly the
same; although it is true that in the theatre
ideas of greatness are never tested against any
very hard or trying standard, and he might
well have been another of those who had simply, with an accidental success, a little luck

and a few shoddy notions, got by, so that I responded to his name with the respect that I usually reserve for those of more solid achievement, for Angus Wilson, for Dr. Leavis and those others who have really done real things.

When he finished speaking, everyone clapped and started to wander around again. I made my way back to the kitchen door for another drink, where I met an old lady who had been on the stage for years and who had clearly found out from experience what I had found out from reason, for she was the only person there who seemed really merry. She winked at me as the butler emerged with another tray, and we deftly helped ourselves; she then made off for the mushroom patties, and I started to look, as I always start to look, for interesting young men. The sad truth was that there was nobody: there were no young men at all except for the actors, and half of them were queer. The handsomest man there was my husband. This discovery did not fill me with pride, but with a fearful restlessness. I did not want to think so ill of human nature, to think that David was the best there was. I watched him from a distance: he was talking to two young and I think unmarried women. I could hear what they were saying: they were saying that they hoped things would liven up a bit now the theatre had come. Then one of them said that she liked David's tie, and started to finger it; he looked at her, and I could feel some imminent gesture.

"If you like it," he said loudly, "you can have it. I don't think much of it myself."

And he thereupon unknotted it from his neck

and handed it to her: a true specimen of one of his gifts. The girl looked overcome with horror.

"No, no," she kept saying, "that isn't what I meant, that isn't what I meant at all, please take it back." She thrust it at him, but he would not take it.

"I'm telling you," he said, "I don't like it, I don't want it. My dear lady, I shall be most offended if you don't take it."

As he insisted, his accent grew broader and his attitude coarser. I could see from the girl's face her fright at being thus involved with what she had not bargained for. She had made an overture only slightly more risky than she would have ventured on in her own society, and it had been picked up and twisted with the rude literal rapidity of which Dave was peculiarly capable. She had thought he was a pleasant young man, quite ready to embark on a little verbal provocation, but instead she had found herself caught up with a crude and solid object, now dangling there in her hand. She did not know what to do with it: her unhappiness seemed to outweigh the small touch of gratification she must have received at having her flippancy so seriously and publicly received. I was annoyed with David. I could see that he had done it deliberately to hurt her; she was not the kind of girl he liked, and he was now making no effort to minimize what he had done. It was irritation, I guessed, that had driven him to the gesture in the first place: he does not like to be fingered or patronized. As far as I can see, he has no right not to like it, for it is on such vicarious fingering that his career depends, but he has always liked to think that he can have the best of both worlds and that he can bite with impunity the hand that strokes him. Actors are like that: they live upon applause, but they cannot bear to see the grinning face above the clapping palms.

Finally the girl rolled the tie up and put it in her bag. I was glad that she had at least got it: perhaps in time it would afford her more pleasure than pain. I did not respect her attitude much more than David's, when all is said: the relationship between audience and performer has always filled me with unease.

I walked off quickly, leaving my barenecked husband to his own social confusion. I had myself opted out, I had hardly spoken a word to anyone, having felt the general pointlessness of engaging in such a dualized gathering. I belonged to neither nation, and to speak was to take sides. I was just wondering whether I ought not to get ready to go back and feed Joseph when two people who bore in every attribute the print of town rather than of theatre came up to me and addressed me. How brave, I thought as I saw them stop before me and open their mouths. And then I realized that I knew them.

"Surely," the woman said, "you must be Emma Lawrence? You won't remember us, I daresay, but you used to come and stay with us years ago in Cheltenham."

"Of course I remember you," I said quickly, and I did. "Mr. and Mrs. Scott, isn't it? And how is Mary? I haven't seen Mary for years."

It all came back to me in one of those filmsequence sweeps of total recall to which I am subject. I had been at school with their daughter, who was for years one of my closest friends. We used to stay with each other during the holidays, to write each other long weekly letters and to share our secrets. And then, since we left school, we had not met or written, except for one occasion in London, when we had lunch together, and had, I thought, mutually realized our total lack of sympathy for each other. Mr. Scott was an extremely well-to-do solicitor and a man of great acidity. I had never dared to converse with him, as he had no scruples about correcting with malicious pleasure the ill-founded notions of fifteen-year-old girls, and although I did not understand the grounds for his corrections, I always understood the malice. Mrs. Scott, on the other hand, was one of those mild-faced professional women whose even features denote a deliberate evenness of life: I remember that despite the lavishness of their means and the careful comfort of their house she managed to avoid any suggestion of extravagance. On the contrary, despite the large prime joints, I always got the impression that their household was governed by a mild and firm economy.

She had not changed at all, and it must have been seven years since I had seen her. Her hair was still the same light crinkled brown, still drawn back into the same low bun on the nape of her neck; and her dress, pale blue and light woollen jersey with a fabric belt, seemed to be the one that I had seen her in so often before. And indeed, it may well have been the same: it was not the kind of dress that dates, or fades, or rots. She looked correct, and it was with a

pang of sadness, as though realizing my age,
that I noticed that I did not much care what
she thought of my hat. I would rather have
burned with shame than have faced her from
such a cool appraising distance, for I used to
admire her, as I had admired her daughter;
and what did I wear such a hat for but to burn
with shame? Later that night I thought that
perhaps I had worn the hat because I liked it;
but then again, perhaps not.

"Mary's married now," said Mrs. Scott,
"didn't you know? It was in *The Times*. She
lives very near us, her husband is a barrister.
They were married last year, didn't you
know? You must be here with the theatre,
aren't you? I never knew that you had gone
on the stage."

"I haven't," I said. "I married an actor, that's
why I'm here. We're here just for the season."

"Oh, then you must see Mary. She lives near
here, we see a lot of her. I must tell her that
I saw you, and perhaps she can call on you
when she's in Hereford."

"That would be lovely," I said.

"And how's your father? Do you see much
of him these days? I see little bits about him
in the paper from time to time. He's still in
Cambridge, isn't he?"

"Oh yes, he's still there. I see him every now
and then."

I wondered whether she would have the
nerve to ask me, in those all-flattering tones,
about my mother, and whether, if she did, I
would respond, as I usually responded, with the
unassimilable phrase "Oh, she died in the end."
I could see her hovering on the brink of

the question, and I could feel myself hovering on the brink of my reply, when Mr. Scott intervened.

"And how long have you been married, Emma?" he said.

I looked at him: he was looking at me with the eyes of calculation, and I saw in him for the first time all kinds of curious features that I had never guessed at before.

"I've been married for four years now," I said.

"You must have married young."

"Not particularly. I was twenty-two."

I felt, in the face of such criticism, that I should say that it was Mary that had married late; and then he went on to:

"And have you any children?" and I saw where he was going. There was no right answer to make: if I had had none, he would have classed me as one of those wicked young things who ignores their social duties and get married to have a good time; and if I confessed to any, unless I crudely stated dates and birthdays, he would assume that I had married at so foolishly young an age through necessity.

"I've two children," I said, "a girl and a boy."

"Well," said Mr. Scott, "how you do grow up."

"How lovely," said Mrs. Scott, returning to her own smooth groove. "I think it must be lovely to have children young, everyone seems to do it nowadays. And how do you manage? You must manage to get about a little or you couldn't even be here now, could you?"

"Oh, I have a French nanny," I said, making a brazen attempt at grandeur: I knew that that

would shock them, I knew that in their scale it
was permissible to spend vast sums on garden-
ers and domestic help and household decora-
tions, but that to have a nanny was as wicked
as to have a chauffeur. "I do need," I said,
following up my assertion, "to get out a little,
especially in a quiet place like this."

"Oh, I think you'll enjoy being here when
the summer comes. It's very lovely, the countryside, and there's all of Wales just on the
doorstep, you know. We live near here ourselves
now, we moved from Cheltenham. When the
family began to grow up and leave home, we
found that big house was really too much
for us. . . ."

And she told me, for the next five minutes,
about how the house had been too much for
her. Unlike her husband, she had no real interest in me. As I watched her talking, I wondered whether it had been the extreme re-
fined ordinariness of her that had attracted me
so much as a child: hers was the kind of face
that could never grow on a woman not born
to professional command. I have seen such
faces on headmistresses, on committee women,
on doctors and dons, and never have I seen
them on the underprivileged. Whereas faces
like my mother's, my vivid, bony mother's, I
have seen on many a barmaid and in many a
back street. I thought about my mother as Mrs.
Scott's voice continued in my ears, telling me
the fortunes of her other children and what
Mary had worn at her wedding. My mother
had been a perpetual invalid, and had suffered
all her life from tuberculosis, which had finally,
the year before my marriage, and when she

was only forty-three, killed her. I had never known her very well: I was a nanny's child, my mother to me was an exotic, miserable woman who lived from time to time in sanatoria and from time to time in bed upstairs at home. From an early age I can remember the lurid pity of others: my father and I seemed to be the only people capable of taking the affair calmly. It was the kind of story that attracts the Mary Scotts of this world: I think now that they must have been perpetually waiting for my own dramatic death, Brontë-fashion, in my little crib at school. Whereas I, in my hard-headed way, and thanks, I now realize, to the behaviour of my remarkable father, had simply lifted from my background what I thought would be of use: an excuse for mild indulgence, a good sob story to endear myself to people late on in parties, a harsh degree of anonymity and a respect for my father. And a certain foreordained distance from and attraction towards people like Mrs. Scott, who had herself, it is quite easy to see, been some sort of mother substitute for me. Not that I wanted a mother like that: I did not, even as a child, but she must have represented for me a regularity that I should have needed. I do not wish to set Mrs. Scott up as an example of anything: she was a kind woman, and I respected the way she had brought up her family and managed her husband. But she left too much out.

My mother, as well as being an invalid, drank. Not heavily, just more than was good for her, or more than would have been good for her had she been able to lead a normal life. I think my father did not try to discourage her. I was wondering, for the first time, if the Scotts had known about this, as they might have done, for Mary had once visited us in Cambridge and seen the gin bottles, when David arrived and interrupted Mrs. Scott's monologue by taking me by the elbow.

"I think we'd better go, Emma," he said when she paused. "I've invited a few of the chaps back for a drink, I couldn't find very much here."

"This is my husband, David Evans," I said, and introduced him to them quickly.

I do not know whom I meant to annoy, but I did not succeed in annoying anyone, for David immediately turned on the charm.

"Old friends of Emma's?" he was saying in no time. "Oh, you must come back and have a drink."

They knew better than to accept, but they were delighted: they discussed the theatre, and me, and I could hardly believe my ears, but in no time he was thanking them for looking after me in my unhappy childhood. At this I thought we should go.

"I think most people have an unhappy childhood," I said crossly, "and now I've got to go and feed Joseph, he'll be yelling his head off."

"Can't the nanny deal with that?" said Mr. Scott, and I looked him in his nasty blue eye and said:

"I believe in breast-feeding, don't you?"

"On top of all that alcohol?" said Mr. Scott, indicating my empty glass. I thought he thought I was lying. I enjoyed my encounter with Mr. Scott.

"She's very naughty," said David, "if she's

been drinking, she's only allowed to drink stout."

"Oh, shut up, for Christ's sake," I said, and walked off, thinking that I had at least given them their money's worth. David remained behind to pacify them, which seemed ironic. I wouldn't have put it past him to tell them that I was sickening myself and to be treated with care.

He caught up with me just as I made my way down the front steps; he was followed by a crowd of six or seven other actors, including, I noticed, Sophy Brent.

"You don't mind if they all come in for a drink, do you?" he said as he overtook me.

"Of course I mind," I said. "I don't know any of them, and we haven't got anything to drink in the house anyway."

"Well, you'll just have to get to know them, won't you?" he said, and dropped back to walk with them behind. I strode on quietly; it was only ten minutes' walk, and they all stopped to buy some drink at an off-license, so I reached home before them. Joseph was indeed yelling his head off in Pascal's arms; she had tried to silence him with orange juice, but had not succeeded. I felt mean: I was only a quarter of an hour late, and I objected to having to feel mean, but I felt it just the same. My children are always making me suffer emotions that have no other sanction than their mere factual existence. I grabbed him from her, sat down in the hard, armless chair that we had brought with us from London for this purpose, ripped open my shirt and let him begin. As instantaneous, greedy silence fell, I thought,

Right, Joe, cow's milk for you tomorrow, and
made a mental note to order another pint. I
then got Pascal to fetch me the list of facts
that I was at that point trying to learn: they
were a lot of dates of events preceding the
Sicilian Vespers, and what charm they then
had for me I cannot now imagine, except for
the charm of relating to what had once, as far
as can be ascertained, occurred, whereas my
feeding of Joseph seemed at times hardly to
be occurring at all. That was his fault: he was,
though ravenous, a lazy child, and I thought
with relief of that sterile bottle, which Pascal
could administer just as well as I could.

After five minutes or so David and his
friends arrived. They had got a crate of beer
and a bottle of whisky. I cannot think of two
more unpleasant drinks, though whisky has, I
suppose, its uses. David introduced me to those
that I did not know: there was Sophy, and
Michael Fenwick again, who looked peculiarly
sick at the sight of Joseph sucking, and a thin
young man called Julian with a pale baby face,
who was so much true to type that I could
hardly distinguish him from the other young
men, so like him, that I had known. I took to
him immediately: his nervous earnest flippancy
reminded me somehow of myself. Then there
was another man, about David's age, who had,
I realized, already established himself as the
company's pain in the neck, for upon introduc-
tion, when I said, "How do you do?" he responded by telling me how he did, by
describing to me in frightening detail the state
of his throat and his liver and his weak ankle.
The others exchanged looks: clearly they had

heard every word of it before. There was not,
I think, anything wrong with him, apart from
the pale stare and loud voice of fanaticism.
The last member of the party was Neville, the
film star, whom David had known for some
time: he was a hot, sloppy-featured, attractive
man, and, unlike David, stupid and, I suspect,
sentimental with it. However, I was glad that
he was there, as he seemed intent upon enjoying himself, whereas the others were an odd
enough collection and could easily have been
plunged in gloom. Also, I could see that the
sight of Joe and myself was almost enough to
distract him from the sight of Sophy Brent:
clearly he was not one to be repelled by the
flesh. Julian, although he did not much like
flesh, was very taken with Joe: he liked babies,
he said, and when Joe had finished feeding he
nursed him for a little.

They all sat round with their drinks, and after the most cursory attention to my existence
they began to talk about acting. I had foreseen this: what else could they have talked
about? They did not know about anything else.
First of all they discussed the plays they were
going to do, and the parts they were going to
play, and what Wyndham Farrar had said to
them about it. They seemed to think that *The
Clandestine Marriage* was quite a good play
and that *The White Devil* was quite awful. I
gathered that Sophy Brent had got a very good
part in the former, as she was playing the clandestine wife, and that she was very lucky to
get it, as she was only just out of drama school.
It was not, naturally, she herself that gave this
away; but I picked it up with no difficulty,

largely I think from the hypochondriac, Don Franklin, who was not so much malicious as totally lacking in any sense of what should, for others' comfort, be revealed or concealed. He lacked this sense with regard to himself as well, it is true to say, and would recount his own humiliations with equally tedious gusto. I also gathered, with regard to Sophy, that Wyndham Farrar had his eye on her; I think I gathered this largely from remarks that she herself let drop, though the other men, or at least Neville and David, had an avid attitude towards her that implied competition. She gave at one point an account of her audition, at Wyndham's house behind Cavendish Square: she said she had done *Gallop apace ye fiery-footed steeds,* and he had told her she was trying to be too virginal. When she spoke, she used one long crowding flow of superlatives, which became after a while exhausting.

When they had finished with parts and personalities and I had put Joseph back into his cot, they started off on the theory of acting. For those who had never heard actors discuss their trade, I may say that there is nothing more painfully boring on earth. I think it is their lack of accuracy, their frightful passion for generality that rob their discussions of interest. They were talking, this time, about that ancient problem of whether one should, while acting, be more aware of the audience or the person or persons with whom one is playing the scene. I must have heard this same argument once a fortnight over the last four years, and never has anyone got a step nearer to any kind of illumination, because instead of talking ration-

ally they just wander round the morasses of
their own personalities, producing their own
weaknesses for examination as though they
were interesting, objective facts about human
nature, which, I suppose, in a way they are,
and that is why I continue to listen. David, of
course, true to his contempt for the paying
public, was taking the line that one should concentrate wholly on one's co-actor, on what is
going on between two people on the stage; he
was being opposed principally by Michael
Fenwick, who was an avowed believer in technique.

"It's all a question of truth," David was saying. "You can't tell the truth if you have one
eye on how it's being taken all the time, can
you? You have to narrow your circle of con-
centration down to the situation you're playing, you can't keep listening for reactions."

"But the whole art of acting," said Michael
Fenwick (and who else but actors ever claim
that acting is an art?) "consists in communication. You have to convey your ideas to the
public, you have to adjust your performance
to what they can take."

"That's just dishonesty," said David, "that's
all that is. You mean that if you're playing Ten-
nessee Williams in Cheltenham you gloss over
all the punch lines for fear of offending the
old ladies. What good does that do anyone?
They don't get a performance, they don't even
get the play. You might as well give them what
you believe to be true, not what you believe
they believe to be true, mightn't you?"

"You seem to forget," said Michael, big,
lumpy Michael, forgetting in an instant his last

statement about art, "that acting is basically
entertainment, the actor isn't there to instruct,
he's there to amuse, and you can't amuse people unless you pay attention to their reactions.
It's like fishing: you give them a bit of line and
see if they're biting, and if they are you give
them a bit more." I do not think that Michael
Fenwick had ever seen a live fish in his life.

"That's just nonsense," said David. "You
must be talking about pantomime or something. What I was talking about was acting. I
must say I've no particular desire to amuse anyone, I just want to get on with it, that's all."

"It's easy to tell," said Michael, "that you're
not used to playing for live audiences. You've
spent all your life in front of cameras, that's
what's the trouble with you. That's what's the
trouble with the theatre these days, people
like Wyndham Farrar keep importing all these
great stars of screen" (glowering at Neville)
"and telly and expect them to be able to turn
out a good stage performance, just like that.
Stage acting is an art, a lost art; it's been
ruined by all you lot who think it's just an easy
way of earning a lot of money."

"What in Christ's name do you think you're
talking about?" said David belligerently.
"Where do you think I started off? Do you
think I began as a BBC extra or something?
I've played in just about every bloody rep in
this bloody country. I'd been at it three years
before I ever saw the inside of a television
studio."

"Three years?" said Michael, who had been
on the stage for twenty. "Three years? Do you
think you can learn anything in three years?"

"Of course you can," said David, "if you've got your wits about you."

I held my breath: I could see him toying with the idea of saying, "I've learned more in three than you in thirty," and I could not bear the prospect of the inevitable ensuing flabby wounded collapse. No more apparently could David, for he went on:

"And what I learned was that you must always, always be yourself. Whether you're playing to fifty in Oldham or five million or fifty million, there's nothing else you have to offer but yourself, so that's what you have to give. And to hell with inflections and upstaging and all that bloody moronic nonsense. That's all a bloody waste of time if you ask me, you can learn all about that in a week in any old rep in England."

Michael was too annoyed to reply immediately, and Julian took up this bristly challenge in a reedy, girlish voice.

"I don't see why," he said, "you should think that yourself is so wonderful. After all, the public pays to see a play, doesn't it, not to see David Evans or—er—or Laurence Olivier."

"They may not *pay* to see David Evans," said David, ignoring as well he might the other example offered, "but that's what they see when they get there just the same, isn't it? And if I can't believe in myself as myself, I don't see what else there is to believe in. I don't want to spend my life covering myself up in wigs and muck. I don't believe acting has anything to do with imitation."

"I can't imagine what you're an actor for then," said Michael, who had gathered enough

ammunition to continue. "If you don't have any
interest in the parts you're playing or the people who are watching you, then what are
you doing it for?"

"Oh, for myself," said David. "For myself.
To discover about me. With each new part I
play, I find out more about me. And if people
will pay to see it, that's their lookout, not
mine."

And so they went on, pointlessly, messily. As
I say, I had heard it all before, but I nevertheless found something touching and pathetic in
David's assertion of his own positive wonderful
self: poor David, who has no more self than a
given quantity of water and who is always trying to contain his own flowing jelly-like shapelessness in some stern mould or confine because
he is, I think, afraid of the aimlessness of his
own undirected violence. I watched him as he
talked: his handsomeness, I now see, consists
almost entirely in the marvellous threatening
smoky parallel between the line of his brow
and the line of his eye, and if I constrict my
attention to this area of his face I can almost
revive in myself that first original passion. In
fact, so effectively did I persuade myself on
to his side that I eventually got up and said
I would go and make some spaghetti as it was
past nine and nobody had yet eaten anything
except those cocktail biscuits at the reception.
David looked surprised and said that it was
very kind of me: he doubtless thought I was
undergoing my usual silent fury. So I went off
into the kitchen to chop up onions. As I
chopped, I thought about the discussions that
I used to hear as a child in my father's house,

about God and the Church and the interpreta-
tion of curious grammatical construction in the-
ological writings. Those discussions, it is true,
had had a fine and detailed precision, but it
had always astonished me that people had
found it possible to talk for so long about the
structure of the Trinity when it seemed far
from clear to me that God was One or indeed
Any, let alone Three. It was that, I think,
amongst other things, that started me off on
my passion for facts and for typed lists about
the Angevin empire. I wanted to know what
could be known. And now I seemed to have
ended up in a society even further removed
from facts than my father's. At least Athanasi-
us and Arius had existed, which was in itself
interesting, even if what they had existed for
was far from certain. But what was the theatre
itself but one huge irrational sham, made for
fantasy and fiction, not for fact? To me it hardly seemed to touch reality at any point; and yet
it existed, like that wardrobe in my bedroom
it existed, and indeed, it existed sufficiently to
provide my bread and butter, my onions and
garlic and my tomatoes in tins.

I had just served the spaghetti out in soup
plates and was looking for the Parmesan when
Sophy appeared in the doorway and asked if
she could help: a well-timed entrance. She was
a little tight: she had been at the whisky, and
she kept one hand on the wall as she watched
me. I must say that she was most amazingly
beautiful. Even standing there she seemed to
fill the kitchen with her lavish bounce. Her skin
against her black dress had an extraordinary
golden full-blooded bloom, like fruit; she had a

technicolor brightness. After watching me in
silence for a few moments she said:

"It really is most frightfully sweet of you to
give us all supper like this, Emma."

"Yes, it is, isn't it?" I said as I pierced holes
in the cheese canister.

"I suppose you must have an awful lot of
people round all the time, don't you?"

"Oh, now and then."

"You know, I'm sure I've seen you somewhere
before. Did you used to be an actress or
something?"

"No, I've never been an actress."

"Don't you ever want to go on the stage,
hearing about it all the time like this? I'm sure
I should if I were married to an actor."

"No, I can't say the idea of being an actress
has ever appealed to me particularly."

"Where is it that I've seen you then? Surely
I must have met you somewhere? At a party
or something?"

"Perhaps," I said, beginning to feel an obscure need to establish myself as something
other than the housewife which she clearly
hoped I might be, "perhaps you've seen my
photograph somewhere. I used to do a little
modelling for the *Coronet.*"

"Not really. Christ." That had gone straight
to her tiny shiny heart, I could see. "I knew you
must have been something, the way you're
dressed. I've never seen such a fantastic blouse,
where on earth did you get it? And what about
that hat you were wearing? I've never seen
anyone in a hat before, nobody I know would
wear a hat."

"Didn't you like it?"

"Of course I liked it. It was the most beautiful hat I've ever seen. I've just never seen one like it before, that's all."

"That's probably because it's about sixty years old," I said, wondering why I should warm to her appreciation: I was confronted once more with the question of audience and performer. And yet the fact that she applauded did in a sense commend her.

"Is it really? Good heavens, no wonder it looked out of this world. And you say you used to do modelling, however did you get in on that? I thought that it was supposed to be a closed world and all that."

"It is a closed world, that's precisely how I did manage to get in on it. I had a friend, you know, who happened to be a good photographer. And all that."

"Lucky you, how terrific. Have you given it up now?"

"I suppose so. Temporarily. After all, there isn't much scope in Hereford, is there?"

"You could travel up and down."

"I have two children," I said, not that I expected the implications to strike home.

"Oh well, yes," she said, "I suppose you must be quite happy in the house, but I couldn't exist for a moment in a place like this unless I were working. I would have died this evening if I hadn't come round here. I can't face the look of my flat, I really can't."

"Perhaps," I said, "you could carry a couple of platefuls through, and we can get started."

"Oh, oh yes," she said, and came away from the wall with a slight swoop. She picked up the nearest two plates and went back into the other

room, where no doubt she sat down to eat one
of them, as she did not come back to carry
any more. And I thought, how pernicious it is,
she is now prepared to respect and dislike me,
to treat me as a serious and possibly harmful
person, and only because she knows that I have
some right to exist in a world which she herself
would not mind entering; whereas if I had had
pretensions to nothing, if I had had no interest
in the theatre, in entertainment, in modelling,
in television, she would have been quite happy
to like me. And I would rather have her dislike
than her affection.

In bed that night, when David had switched
out the light and we were each of us lying still
in our private churning silences, I said to him,
"David, did you mean all that about being
yourself? Do you really think that it's enough,
just to struggle on at being yourself?"

"What else can I do?" he said. "I don't see
what else I *can* do. If I don't be what I am, then
I'm not being anything. And if what I am isn't
good enough, then I'd better find out, hadn't
I? If I fall off somewhere, I want to know where.
I don't want just to get by."

"But, Dave," I said, reaching out and taking
his hand, "how can it be as simple as that? I
know you're serious about being an actor, I
know you want to be a good actor, I know
that's why we're here, but surely if you take
being an actor seriously you ought to pay some
attention to what other actors, you know, the
great actors, have done?"

"I don't see why."

"Don't you? I don't know about acting, but
I feel that if I wanted to write a book, for in-

stance, or paint, then I would try to pay some
attention to what—well, what Henry James or
Titian had done. Or not done."

"And what good would that do you?"

"I don't know. Doesn't it do one good to set
oneself a high ideal?"

"I don't think so," said David. "I just don't
think so. If you're not a Henry James then it
won't do you any good to think about him, and
if you are then you won't need to. I don't think
there is a higher ideal than myself, personally.
I'm quite prepared to think that I'm the best actor in the country. In fact, it's necessary to think
so; all it means is that I'm the best one of me
that there is."

"You are the best," I said, and nibbled at the
ends of his fingers.

"You wouldn't think so," he said, "from the
way that you treat me."

"What do you mean? I gave you and your
horrid friends a lot of nice supper, didn't I?"

"That's not what I mean," he said, tightening
his grasp on my knuckles until it hurt.

"You won't get anywhere by force," I said,
pulling away.

"That's the only way I do get anywhere," he
said. "I've had two children by force, haven't
I?"

"It's legalized rape," I said, and he let go my
hand and turned over on his side, taking the
sheets and blankets with him. And I turned
my own thin spine towards him, and so we
fell asleep.

5

THE next morning I gave Joseph his first bottle
of cow's milk. He drank it all, with far less fuss
than he used to display when I fed him myself,
so I was glad that the idea of weaning him had
occurred to me. I was suddenly very anxious
for my breasts to return from their tight,
round, full inhuman globes to their usual small
selves. I had had enough of maternity. I was
sucked dry.

When I had finished with Joseph, I left him
and his sister with Pascal and went into town to
do the shopping. I had arranged to meet David
at the theatre at lunchtime, and before I did so
I intended to organize myself and this town. I
was ready to walk for miles to find the right
butcher and the right grocer. After an hour's
investigation, when I had fixed myself up with
everything except a large tin of oil, I began to
panic: it was a strange feeling to notice that I
was so out of my depth, that there was nothing
and no one in the town to which I could relate
myself. With deprivation and a sense of loss
I made my way to the nearest Wimpy Bar and
ordered a cup of coffee, for the decor in these
places is the same, the coffee tastes the same in
Hereford as in London, and, who knows, they

may have them, too, in Buenos Aires and Beirut. I felt at home there, as I feel in Marks and Spencers; or rather not at home, but unnoticed in the anonymous brightly painted delocalized calm. And there, sure enough, was a small group of actors, who had made their way there with the same birdlike instinct: all those who were not working that morning. In a week or two, in fact, they discovered another coffee bar, nearer to the old narrow streets where we lived, which had some pretension to an arty student life, and they took it over. They simply moved in. They did not drive everyone else out, because some remained to stare, but they must have ruined the place for its local long-haired personalities forever.

When I had had my coffee and found my tin of oil, which I could not get delivered, I set back over the bridge to the theatre. I was near enough, but the tin banged against my knees as I walked. When I arrived at the stage door, there was no sign of David, or of anyone else, so I started to read the notices on the notice-board, assuming that the company had not yet broken for lunch. I read the cast lists, and who was understudying whom, and notices about not parking cars in the public car park; then I started to arrange all the spare drawing pins in a neat circle. As I was doing this, someone arrived behind me. I did not turn, but became increasingly aware that whoever it was, was not moving. After a minute or so the person said:

"Do you think I might disarrange your nice little pattern and have a couple of pins?" and I turned round and saw that it was Wyndham

Farrar with a piece of paper that he wanted to pin up.

"I suppose so," I said, unpicking two and offering them to him. "They are hardly mine to withhold."

"No, I didn't think they would be," he said, taking the pins, but not doing anything more about it. "I didn't think you would have anything to do with these drawing pins. Though what you have got anything to do with I can't imagine. You're not in my company, are you? I can hardly have engaged an actress looking like you without having noticed it."

"I am not an actress!" I said irritably. In London nobody ever mistakes me for an actress, but I could see what my fate in this place was to be.

"I didn't think you could be," he said. "If you had been, I would have met you before."

"You have met me before, as a matter of fact," I said. "But clearly you don't remember."

"I'm quite sure you're mistaken," he said. "I'm quite sure I've never met you anywhere."

I wondered how far he would go if I allowed him. I felt that it might be quite a long way, I felt it my duty to end the walking misrepresentation which is myself.

"Oh, I remember the occasion quite well," I said. "It was all most unfortunate, in my opinion. It was at a party of Danny Owen's. I was there with my husband."

"Your husband?"

"David Evans, my husband."

"Oh," he said. "Oh yes. Really. David Evans.

I didn't know he was married. He doesn't seem
to be particularly married. Was I introduced
to you? Come to think of it, I did know about
David; he told me some long story about having
a wife and a lot of kids to support when the
subject of salary came up. But I didn't know
he was married to anyone like you."

"How should you have known? It would
hardly have been relevant, would it?"

"Oh, I don't know about that. Most things
come in handy, one way or another. When he
told me that story, I thought that if it was
true then he probably had a very homely wife.
A lot of these people do, you know."

"What people?"

"People like David. Why did you say that our
meeting, which for some extraordinary reason
I cannot recollect, was unfortunate?"

"Only because I assume that if you hadn't
met David then you wouldn't have thought of
asking him to be in your company, and if you
hadn't asked him then we wouldn't be here.
What I really mean is, I wouldn't be here."

"Then you don't like it here?"

"For what conceivable reason should I like it
here?"

"It's a very healthy spot, you know. Fresh air.
Cows. What more do you want?"

"I can think of a thing or two."

"Anyway, it's very unfair of you to say that
the thought of your husband would never have
crossed my mind if I hadn't seen him at that
party. I think he's a very good actor, don't
you?"

"Naturally."

"You know, Mrs. Evans," said Wyndham Farrar, using this term of address with some sinister intent, "you can say what you like, but I'm sure you must be an actress. I know I've seen your face somewhere before. No, no, I don't mean at Danny Owen's party. I've seen you somewhere else."

"Oh no you haven't," I said. "I can assure you that you haven't. I would have remembered if you had. I remember everything."

"And you're not an actress?"

"No. Certainly not."

"I can't imagine why you're not an actress. You look as though you ought to be an actress," he said perseveringly, and I said:

"The stage doesn't interest me, I'm just not interested," and I started to move away: already I could feel the pointless wheels in that piece of dud machinery beginning to turn, that dud machine, which, like a failed effort at perpetual motion, will tick for a little and then stop and stick and rust.

"Well," he said, "be that as it may, and whatever your interests, and I'm sure that you must have some, I expect I shall see more of you in the next few months. After all, you have to be friendly in a place like this, don't you? In such a small town?"

"You could see it that way," I said, irresistibly turning from the green baize of the noticeboard to meet, for the first time, his attention: a mistake, my first real mistake, for there was, I thought, in his eyes and the ugly map of his face the kind of intention to which I am incapable of saying no, the kind of domineering, warlike intention that stiffens me throughout.

Having encountered my gaze, he thought he had said either enough or too much, and I wished I knew which; then he started to pin up his notice. It said, *Could I see Sophy Brent in my office at five thirty this afternoon.* When I had taken this in, I was relieved from further talk or silence by the arrival of the entire company, who had clearly just been released from some mass talk by one of Wyndham's inferiors. I was swept off to eat pork pies in a pub with David and Neville and Julian and one or two others. As I munched mouthfuls of stale dry pastry, I tried to decide whether I had been shaken, whether I was still shaking; it seemed to me that I must be or the question would not have been in my mind. I could not think what it was that could have so affected me, for I meet a lot of people, and many of them are rude or gallant or impertinent or suggestive upon indiscriminate principle, quite flippantly, with no thought or intention of consequences, and I had no reason to assume that Wyndham Farrar was not just such another, as casual and possibly less appreciative than a man whistling from a passing lorry. And yet, knowing this and expecting nothing, I nevertheless felt shaken, as though what he had said had been said to me myself, and not to David Evans' wife, or to a woman looking at a noticeboard who seemed from the eccentricity of her hair style to be an actress.

I suppose, in view of the consequences, that the only odd thing was that this should have been technically our second meeting and not our first. I have always paid great attention to chronology, and I sometimes wonder these days whether there can have been any significance in the meaninglessness of our first pregnant encounter. First encounters are of such appalling importance. The first time I saw David was not on that train, not even in the lift, but on the television a year before, not knowing who he was and not remembering until after we were married that I had seen him: one day he started to describe to me a certain play that he had done, and I suddenly realized that I had seen it and him, and had thought even at the time that David was the kind of man that would do. When I discovered that it had been him all the time that I had seen and wanted, I was both pleased and disappointed: pleased at the consistency of my judgement, disappointed that there should be one man where I had had a hopeful memory of two.

There is nothing new in this kind of filtered experience: in the theatre there are numerous classical examples of men and women who have fallen in love with actors or actresses from their image on the screen, and on occasion married them. It is not even surprising, for if an actor spends his life making love to the audience what can he expect but that from time to time love is the charge they will bring up against him? And I have since discovered that where Wyndham Farrar first saw me was not at Danny Owen's party, nor at the Garrick Theatre noticeboard, but on the cover of a glossy fortnightly, posed in a brown wool dress against autumn and the Albert Memorial. I looked up the copy, a week ago, just to make sure that I was right, and there in that issue was a long and glowing review of Wyndham Farrar's production of *The Master Builder* at the Gala. Sometimes thoughts of sale and merchandise flit horribly across my heart.

In the pub that lunchtime, as I thought about Wyndham, I talked to Julian: he told me about his parts, and that they were not very good, and that he did not want to spend his life playing boy princes and younger brothers.

"I just happen to look young," he said, "but I'm not really that kind of person at all. It's just the shape of my face," he said sadly.

I found him very appealing: he reminded me of something immensely familiar and reassuring, and when he happened to tell me that his father lectured in English literature at Bristol, I suddenly saw what it was. "My father, too, is a don," I said, and we exclaimed with excitement and compared our backgrounds, dominated as they had been by the well-bred, the quietly discursive, the mildly permissive. He did not seem to have a very precise grasp of the difference that was the theatre, he had not got beyond the fact that his father did not appear to understand that some actors are queer, and that not all actors play all parts, and that some people are destined for a life of juvenile leads.

"He just doesn't seem to see any of the real problems," said Julian plaintively, and although I knew he was being thus plaintive only because I was a woman and ready to listen, I listened. "He doesn't seem to realize," said Julian, "what one is in for."

"I find the same thing in my father," I said, because I had not had occasion to say it for a

long time. "I never know whether it's ignorance or innocence. I never know whether he
really knows or whether he really doesn't
know."

"Exactly," said Julian. "That's exactly what
I mean." And then he thought for a moment,
and turned his large disingenuous eyes upon
me, a whole battery of purity. "Doesn't know
what?" he said.

Oh, I liked him very much, that fleshless,
neatly split boy. Why could I not have someone like him instead? When I got home I
found that I had left my olive oil in front of the
noticeboard, and I had to return in the afternoon to collect it. I do not often forget things in
that way.

6

IN THE first fortnight my life in Hereford settled
down into what should have been its pattern.
Shopping, mornings with Flora and Joseph in
the parks, the odd lunch in a pub with actors,
evenings with actors or the television and the
occasional half hour in the theatre waiting for
David and watching rehearsals that had over-
run. David was very busy: he was rehearsing
for two plays at once, one for Wyndham and
one for an ineffectual man called Selwyn. He

was often out during the evenings as well as
during the day, working or talking. I was glad
to see him preoccupied: mean I am, but not so
mean, and I know the pleasure of preoccupa-
tion. I began to regret, though I would not admit it, that we had not taken the new house with
the garden, because there was nowhere to
leave Joseph in his pram, except in the downstairs garage, which faced directly onto the
street and occupied what ground floor our
house possessed. I should have made clear that
the whole of our house was on the first floor:
it had been two houses, now knocked into one,
and under one side there was this garage, and
under the other some locked and unexplained
place which must have been a warehouse. Poor
Joseph spent his day street-watching in this garage, amongst the packing cases, or being
pushed by Pascal or me.

I find it takes very little time for me to become thoroughly bored. To me life seems to be
perpetually on the verge of extinction, which
in view of my childhood is natural, and I could
bear anything rather than to die in a moment
of boredom. I feel that I am insulting something
when I am bored. I began to miss London: it
was not so much that I had many close friends
there, for I have few friends, but I missed
variety. My tastes are shallow, my life is shallow,
and I like anonymity, change and fame. In
Hereford, I could have none of these things: I
was condemned to familiarity, which beyond
anything I find hard to maintain with ease.
There seemed to be nobody in the company
that I would like and no opportunity to meet
anyone out of it, apart from the girl who handed

me my books in the public library. It was not that
I disliked people like Julian, but my appreciation of them hardly passed the aesthetic. Also I
was continually aware that he and everyone
else were leading a life of absorbing, passionate
tension, in which a chance compliment from
Wyndham Farrar at a rehearsal could create
delusions of splendid joy. Wyndham Farrar was
another matter, but he was a busy man and my
husband's employer, and not to be met casually
in Boots or the pub. He passed me once, during
the second week, in his car, as I was walking
over the bridge with the pram to the river gardens, and he slowed down and stared and gestured with his hand as though wishing to suggest something, but the car was too large and
too fast for me to grasp his suggestion.

I told myself from time to time that things
would improve once the season began and that
people would come down from London to visit
us and to see the plays. But it did not much con-
sole me. The only occasion on which I did try
to arrange a small outing for David and myself
turned out to be a fiasco: we had a letter one
morning from a Welsh friend of David's, saying
that he was coming to the Oxford Playhouse to
do a show, and could he come over to see us one
evening. He was one of David's more trouble-
some acquaintances, and evenings with him
usually ended with breakages, but to please
David and because I myself felt in need of a
little cheap riot I said that I would be delighted
to see him, so we fixed an evening, and David
said that he would ask Neville and one or two
others round for a meal. As the day drew near,
I began to look forward to this chap's arrival

with unusual interest: although he was himself
an actor, at least he would presumably talk
about things other than *The White Dèvil, The
Clandestine Marriage,* Wyndham Farrar, the
dressing room facilities and whether Sophy
Brent could act or not. Then, on the morning
of the day that I was expecting him, just as I
was busy separating endless eggs for a mousse,
the telephone rang. I answered it: it was one of
the secretary girls from the theatre, and she
asked me if I could give David a message,
which was to remind him to bring his record of
Dowland along to rehearsal with him that evening. I said yes without thinking, being used to
such messages, and then I took in what she had
said.

When I asked her what was in fact happening that evening, she said that as far as she
knew Wyndham had arranged for several of the
company to go round to his flat to discuss the
music with a man from London and that this
had been fixed up several days ago. When she
rang off, I tried to get hold of David at the theatre, but they told me he was rehearsing somewhere in a church hall; they gave me the telephone number, but when I got through he was
unavailable, so I decided I would have to go
round and confront him in person. I left my
mousse and collected Flora, who had while I
was on the telephone cracked three more eggs
and dropped them, shells and all, into my bowl
of egg white; then we set off. When we arrived
at the church hall, David was in the middle of
a scene, so I said I would wait for him. I took
Flora with me into a little anteroom, which
was full of dusty books. I looked at the titles

while I was waiting: they were a wonderful non-conformist collection, ranging from *The Meaning of Suffering* and *The Narrow Path to God* to the lives of minor missionaries. As I looked at them, I heard sounds of altercation drifting through to me from the rehearsal.

"For Christ's sake," my husband was saying, "if you don't *tell* me what it's like, what on earth can I do about it?" and I could hear Selwyn's faint, detached voice replying:

"My dear David, you must take it for granted that if I don't tell you it's wrong then it's all right."

"It's not all right, it's bloody awful," David shouted helplessly, but clearly to no avail: Selwyn was not sufficiently interested to continue the argument, and they started to go over the scene again. When it was over, I went and stood in the doorway and tried to attract David's attention. Finally, after a lot of angry muttering in a corner with a girl called Viola, he looked round and caught sight of me and came stamping over. I led him out into the ante-room, and instead of asking me what I was doing there he launched into a violent attack on Selwyn.

"The man oughtn't to be allowed near a theatre," he kept saying as he sat down on the small brown wood table and took Flora absent-mindedly into his arms, "he's no more idea of what a director ought to do than— All we ever do is run through the bloody thing time and time again, and he just sits there on his backside smiling like an idiot, and then if anyone complains he says, 'Well, what are your ideas about it then?'."

I sympathized as best I could, and when he had calmed down a little he managed to look at me and said, "I didn't expect to see you here, did you get bored or something?"

"No," I said a little flatly. "I just wanted to ask you what you were doing this evening."

"This evening? Let me think, this evening. Oh yes, I know, I've got to go round to Wyndham's and sing songs, he wants to record some stuff for the Webster thing."

"Does it have to be this evening?" I asked, realizing that it was not even worth sounding plaintive, and he suddenly remembered.

"Oh Jesus," he said. "I know. Hugh. It's today Hugh's coming over, isn't it?"

"That's right."

"Oh God, what a bloody nuisance. I forgot all about it. I can't put Wyndham off now, he's fixed it with everyone else, and anyway, I'm the only person who can sing. Oh God, what a bore. When did Hugh say he'd be coming?"

"He said he hoped he'd get here on the train that gets in just before seven."

"Oh well then, that's not too bad," said David, thinking of a solution, "he can come along to Wyndham's with me for the evening. Wyndham won't mind, he's a very sociable chap, is Wyndham. Then you won't even have to bother getting supper for us, will you? We can get a pie at the pub or something."

"I thought you invited Neville and Viola."

"Oh yes, so I did. Never mind, I'll put them off, shall I?"

"Yes, I suppose so."

"You don't mind, do you, Emma?"

"No, I don't mind."

"You don't like Hugh much anyway do you?"

"No. I mean yes. Yes, I do quite like Hugh."

"Oh well, never mind, he can come again some other time," David said, and just as I was trying to work up the energy to think of some cold remark like "And what am I expected to do for the evening?" Viola appeared and said that Selwyn was looking for David and wanted to run through the corridor scene again.

"Bloody hell," moaned David, thrusting Flora back into my arms, "that's the fifteenth bloody time this morning, and it's exactly the same as when we started."

And he disappeared into the hall once more. I did not see him again until he got into bed with me at two o'clock the next morning. I spent the rest of the day wondering whether I was annoyed or not and whether his forgetfulness had or had not been a serious matrimonial offence. I decided finally as I sat watching the television with Pascal and eating three helpings of chocolate mousse that I was not annoyed at all. I did not expect him to remember, and I did not blame him when he forgot. What I did feel, and this was quite a different matter, what I did feel was envy. A more serious affair than annoyance, though not perhaps so much to my discredit.

After this I made no artificial attempts to keep any kind of social life of my own going. I fell back heavily and silently on my dignity and my resources. Then one afternoon, about three weeks after our arrival, when I was sitting alone at home, I had a visitor. Flora and Joseph had gone with Pascal to the theatre gardens: she was enamoured of the theatre in a true, old-

fashioned style, and would hang around in the
garden outside for hours saying hello to actors
as they came and went. They were happy to say
hello to Pascal: she was a pretty girl. In their
absence I was trying to feed the munching jaws
of my mind by reading an Italian novel, and
was just looking for the dictionary when the
doorbell rang. I could not think of anyone that
it was likely to be, and I felt excited as I went
downstairs to open the door; but when I got
there it was my old school friend Mary Scott.
We stared at each other for too long a hostile
instant, and then she said nervously and gaily:

"Why, Emma, you haven't changed a bit."

"Mary," I said, "how nice to see you, what a
surprise," and I remembered just in time not to
try to kiss her cheek. I had grown so accustomed
to cheek-kissing that I could think of no other
way of greeting her. I could not offer her my
hand, so we stood there, looking at each other,
until I said, "Do come in," and added as an
afterthought, "You haven't changed at all
either."

And she had not, whereas if there is anything
that I had done since I had seen her it was to
change. I knew why she had said what she had
said: it was to disarm me to try to prevent me
from displaying any alarming symptoms of mu-
tation, and she had succeeded, for I had
remembered about the kissing. I had remembered, as she spoke, that the Scotts never used
to touch one another or anyone. As she followed
me through the dingy garage to the foot of the
narrow, carpetless, exposed staircase, I filled
slowly with panic and unease: it was so like me
to live upstairs when other people live down-

stairs, and she had never approved in me the
vein of perversity that had started to show itself even in school. We had been great friends,
and no mistake, and yet everything in me that
was to flourish had belonged to the side of me
from which she had always edged away. She
had always distrusted, for instance, my university background. I used at times to regale my
school friends with what I then considered to be
rich anecdotes about young men I had met who
lived on bread for a whole month, or wore
wooden clogs, or could not get out of bed in the
mornings because they had been reading
Berkeley and were no longer sure that the floor
was there. I could usually get a good audience,
and I was myself enthusiastic about these oddi-
ties. It used to hurt me that Mary would never
take my part and theirs. She would disapprove,
though mildly: she would say that in her opinion
really interesting people did not behave oddly,
that oddness was simply a sign of insecurity,
that true intelligence could satisfy itself perfectly well by orthodox means. I knew all too well
what she meant. And now I felt such a resur-
gence of those old anxieties, for her opinion
did seem to carry weight; and I felt that everything about me, the style of my hair, the furnish-
ings of my house, the nature of my husband's
profession, the nature of my own intermittent
profession, even, as I have said, the fact that my
drawing room was on top of a garage laid me
wide open to censure.

When we reached the top of the stairs, I
showed her into our drawing room, which
looked to me for an instant like a junk shop.
She sat down in one of the chairs belonging to

the three-piece suite which had come, as they
say, with the house. It was a respectable piece
of furniture, and I wished I had not draped it
in a piece of red velour which had once been
one of my father's study curtains. She did look
so exactly the same as she had always looked
that I wondered why I had not thought of her
remark first. She had light brown, naturally
curly hair and one of those small-featured,
smiling faces which are thought tremendously
pretty at school, in one's home town and on
the Continent, and she had not altered by a
hair or a wrinkle. She wore a little powder on
her nose, a little pale pink and very nice lipstick and a yellow-and-grey check skirt with a
grey jersey.

"Well, Mary," I said, "what a surprise to see
you. After all this time."

"I thought my parents told you that I might
be dropping in."

"They did say I might be seeing you, but you
know how it is, how one says things—it must
be years since we saw each other. How long is
it now? Six years?"

"I suppose it must be." She did not bashfully
exclaim at the sound of those six years, but my
heart shrank.

"I haven't seen you," I said, "since you were
in your first year at university. Do you remember that day we met in London? We went to
see some film or other. What was it that we
went to see? Wasn't it Olivier's *Hamlet*? I'm
sure it was, I remember thinking that it was
quite frightful."

"I've no idea," she said. "I never remember

things like that. You always had a good memory."

"That's true."

I started to rock myself gently backwards
and forwards on the rocking chair on which I
was sitting; I was almost overcome by this
strange and skeletal indictment. For it was
true: I always had had a good memory.

"And now you're married," I said, for the
want of anything better to say. "I don't think
your parents told me what your husband's
name was."

"Summers. Henry Summers."

"So now you're Mrs. Summers? Mary Summers. That's a very nice name. A lot better than
mine. Emma Evans I ended up, you know."

I pulled a face, but she did not like me to
care about names, and perhaps in any case the
lack of euphony did not strike her.

"We used to talk at school," she said, "about
when we would get married. If we would get
married. Do you remember? And Mummy told
me that you had two children. I never used to
picture you with children, somehow."

"No, neither did I," I said, looking round for
some confirmation of my children's existence
and finding none but *The Tale of Peter Rabbit*
under my chair. I bent down, picked it up and
placed it conspicuously on the arm of the settee. "They've gone for a walk in the park," I
said, "with the girl."

"You must have been married for a long
time," she said, and I laughed, and said:

"Oh yes, years and years and years."

Then we were silent once more, and looked
at each other. I was already beginning to wor-

ry because there was nothing for tea, and for
what occasions but this should one always have
a cake in the cupboard? When we reopened
conversation we talked about what we had
each done since we had left school: how she
had gone to London University, not that she
particularly wanted to at first, but because her
father had insisted, and had got a good degree
in history and had then done a Diploma of
Education and taught for a year or two in a
good girls' boarding school in the North of England; how I had gone to Italy and lived in
London and done nothing at all. I did not dare
to tell her about my aspirations towards glossy
photographs and television screens. I could see
now, in the cool useful light of her eyes, how
paltry, vain and valueless all such desires truly
were, being nothing but an extension of that
undergraduate longing for notoriety and dis-
ruption with which I had alienated her so many
years before. She did say, at one point:

"I always thought you would go to university
after that year abroad, you were always so
good at the things you liked doing."

But I could not take it upon myself to explain
why I had not bothered to go. It did cross my
mind as we talked that our lives had turned out
quite neatly upside down: she was to have had
the early marriage and the children, I was to
have had the independent and faintly intellectual career. I wondered what had turned us
over: ourselves, the world or accident.

Mary also touched, quite quietly, just as I
was thinking that I would have to go and pro-
duce from nowhere some tea, upon the subject
of my mother.

"I never heard," she said, "what happened about your mother. I saw Sylvia just before she left London, and she didn't know either."

"Oh, she died," I said. "Four years ago, just before I was married."

"Oh? I am sorry to hear that," said Mary, unruffled, but tender and sincere. "I really am sorry. But after all that time it must have been something in the way of a happy release."

"Oh yes," I said briskly, "it was a blessing in disguise, no doubt about it." And then I wished that I hadn't, because she blushed, and looked confused, and said:

"Well, it was only a phrase, I know it's different for you when you're involved, but it still is the kind of a thing that can't drag on forever, isn't it?"

"Oh, I do mean it," I said, "I do mean it. It *was* a blessing in disguise, I can tell you. The night after she died, my father—I don't know" —and I looked for another weighty, serious cliché—"my father seemed ten years younger. He really did. It would have killed him, too, if it had gone on any longer. And now I'll go and make us a cup of tea."

"Oh, please, don't bother, not for me," she said, but she sat back and waited, and I went off into the kitchen, trying to recall with accuracy what the Scotts used to have for tea, all that time ago. I could remember sandwiches, and cake, and biscuits—I thought I had a packet of biscuits—and oh yes, thinly sliced bread and butter, and jam in cut glass dishes. Rapidly I started to slice bread and butter, and to put jam in jam dishes, of which I happened to have two, though David had always used them as

ashtrays. Indeed, it had never occurred to me
before what they could be; but now, shining
bright and full of apricot and black currant
jam, I suddenly saw them for what they were. I
had just discarded a second slice of too thinly
cut bread, which had lost its crumb, when the
doorbell once more rang. Once more my heart
turned over, for I was expecting one person
and one person only, and if the first ring had
not been for him, then the second must be; but
it was not, it was Sophy Brent.

"Hello, darling," she said. "I just thought I'd
drop in. You don't mind, do you? You're not
doing anything, are you? I'm at such a loose
end, when I'm not rehearsing there's nothing
to do at all, is there? I've seen both the films
once. I can't very well go and see them again,
can I? Elvis Presley and *The Flight of Hannibal.* Have you seen *Hannibal?* It's jolly good
really, there's some fabulous bits where the ele-
phants all fall down a precipice, and a smashing Italian girl with the biggest bust you ever
saw, who gets captured or something"—and
as she arrived at the top of the stairs and saw
Mary through the open door—"Oh gosh, I
didn't know you'd got anyone here, I'm not disturbing you, am I?"

"Not at all," I said. "This is Mary Summers,
an old school friend of mine. Mary, this is
Sophy Brent."

"Hello," they both said, and as I excused
myself to make the tea I heard Sophy rushingly
continue.

"I *hate* meeting old school friends," she was
saying. "I can never think of what to say to

them, and I can never remember people's
names. . . ."

After a few unpunctuated sentences Mary
broke in to suggest that Sophy must be an
actress; it was the first time she had mentioned
the theater since she had arrived. With this
opening, Sophy proceeded to tell her all about
The Clandestine Marriage, the tea in the green
room, Wyndham Farrar, drama school and
what she referred to as "Emma's fabulous sen-
sational super husband." When I arrived with
the tray and was officially part of the conversation, she said to me in a gaily broad Welsh
accent:

"And where has he got to, that wicked husband of yours? I know he's not at the theatre
because I've just come from there myself, indeed I have."

"I think he's at Peter Yates's," I said. "I think
they're going over the Flamineo-Brachiano
scenes together."

"My God," said Sophy, and I wished she
wouldn't, "they do go at it, don't they. Talk
about a hive of industry, I've never met anything like it."

And so she chattered on, with no apparent
awareness that Mary might not find such gossip
as enthralling as she herself did. I watched
them helplessly, unable to control this social
event which had sprung so unexpectedly upon
me. Sophy might have been a walking symbol
of an actress: she had every manifestation possible, the long loose hair, the smart clear
clothes, the thick mascara, the painted nails,
the talk, the lovely figure and the lovely face.
And the stupidity. There could be no doubt

about it, she came across as stupid and as shiny
as an apple; and she treated me with such darlings and such familiarities that I knew that
Mary must take her for one of my chosen
friends. I could not deny, moreover, that I
found her manner considerably nearer home
than I found Mary's. I had become so accustomed to a bright and superficial flow that I
had to make an effort even to hear its absurdity.
I tried hard not to side with Sophy; I tried not
to side with either of them, I tried to balance
myself neatly in the middle, and I thought, as
I often used to think, though more rarely these
days, of that fable, Aesop's no doubt, in which
a boy and his father and a donkey set off on a
journey and cannot satisfy any passerby that
they are rightly employed. "Oh, the poor
child," cries one as the father rides, and "Oh,
your poor old father," cries another as the boy
rides, and "Oh, the poor donkey," cries a third
as they both ride, and "Oh, what fools to walk
and to take no advantage of your donkey," cries
a fourth as they both dismount, and these are
the cries that echo regularly and more or less in
sequence in my ears.

Sophy was clearly a one to ride her donkey:
she ate everything within sight, spreading far
more jam on her bread than I ever think decent
in company, dropping crumbs and talking all
the time, largely about herself. Mary, on the
other hand, seemed to be soberly walking: she
ate little and talked little, and I remembered as
I watched her that she had always been given
to undue consideration of the feelings of others.
She allowed Sophy to run away with the conversation entirely: she was too well mannered

even to betray any lapse of attention, which
with someone of Sophy's calibre would not anyway have been noticed. She would always remember to shut gates, and would carry orange
peel for miles rather than drop it in a ditch. I
used to say, sometimes, that surely orange peel
would rot, and she would rebuke me and say
that anyone with a real respect for the countryside would never say such things.

After half an hour I began to long for the
children to come back: they would have created a diversion, and have drowned what conversation there was. But it was a fine afternoon,
and they took their time. I grew increasingly
confused as my ear gradually attuned itself to
the differences of phrasing, vocabulary, sentiment and subject matter that separated my two
guests. I began to notice things that I would
never otherwise have noticed: that Sophy's
every other word was Christ, and that Mary's
strongest adjective was awfully; that Sophy
talked solely to impress, and Mary solely and
self-effacingly to communicate; that Sophy's
only idea of a joke was to make some absurd
sexual innuendo about anything she happened
to mention, and that such jokes seemed to her
to be necessary, whereas Mary did not seem to
think that conversation need be in any way
amusing. I think the end had been more or less
reached when Sophy started to recount some
episode with Michael Fenwick and Julian in
rehearsal the day before.

"Christ, it was funny," she was saying.
"There was Julian dozing around as usual, all
weak and floppy, you know what he's like,
when Selwyn says, 'Come on, Julian, try to get

a bit more life into it, try to get a move on,' so
on comes Julian with his chin in the air and his
hands on his hips, trying to look manly, and,
anyway, the first thing Michael had to say in
that scene was 'Look, here comes the sole object
of my desire,' meaning me of course, but of
course when he said it Julian turned round,
and 'Do you mind?' he said. 'We all know . . .' "
and at that moment Flora, whose progress up
the stairs I had been following with bated
breath, rushed in and won the race, so that Julian's wonderful piece of repartee was lost
forever.

I was delighted to see Flora: she sat on my
knee and told them about the ducks and the
swings and the river, and they remarked on her
beauty and intelligence, as they had to. I
would have been very annoyed had they
omitted their duty in this respect. And when
Pascal arrived, Mary asked her many intelli-
gent questions about where she came from,
how she found England and how she was getting on with the English language. Pascal was
very pleased, as not many of our friends had
the social composure to pay her the right kind
of attention, and Mary's middle-class courtesy
was exactly what she did not get enough of.

Finally they left. Mary went first, leaving her
address. Sophy sat it out a few minutes longer,
but in the end she, too, went as I began to mention Flora's bath and Joseph's supper. They left
me thinking.

I remembered, that night, three things. The
first happened when I went on a seaside holiday with the Scott family; family holidays
were of course out of the question for me, and I

was delighted when Mary invited me to go
with them. We went to Devon, and we used to
swim a lot, every day, all weathers; and Mrs.
Scott would be frightened because I insisted on
swimming out of my depth. I used to swim just
straight out, as far as I dared go, and then back
again. For no reason: just for the fright of it.
And she said to me one day:

"You know, Emma, it's very silly to go out of
your depth just for the sake of it, you can swim
just as well, you can have just as nice a time
when you're in shallower water. There's no
need to go out of your depth just to prove you
can do it, you know. We can all see just as well
if you swim along nicely parallel to the shore.
A trapeze artist isn't any the better because he
hasn't got a safety net, you know. It's the skill
that counts, whatever the risk. The risk has
nothing to do with it. It's just as much fun in
your depth as out of it." And I had said, "I
know you're right," but I knew even at that
time that it was not and never would be so;
that I was no professional, that I could ap-
prentice myself to no skill, that I was not one of
the professional classes. The empty water, simply because it was empty water, was what I
wanted: empty water, no matter how far down
you reach, and no foothold.

The second thing I remembered happened in
their house in Cheltenham. It was a big house,
and well organized, with polished wood and
polished floors and carpets, with a drawer for
each set of knives and a special place on a
special shelf for each jam dish and gravy boat.
Usually I slept in Mary's room, but one year, I
forget why, I was put in the small spare room.

Just before I went to bed on the first night, I had a good look round, opening all the drawers and cupboards I could see: they were all empty and neatly lined with spare wallpaper, except for the last one I opened. I had expected to find nothing at all in any of them, but in the last drawer, which was the one in the bottom of the wardrobe, I came across a quite amazing collection of old junk. There were old broken dirty shoes, a greasy old recipe book, bottles half full of patent medicines whose brands no longer existed, a broken bedpan, a large moth-eaten embroidered pincushion, a lot of shoe trees, some plugs and bits of wire and two beer bottles. I could not have been more surprised if I had truly found a skeleton.

The third memory was aroused by a remark that Mary had made about her expectation that I would have gone on to university, or at least to some other kind of education. As indeed, considering myself, I would have expected, too. I tried to trace back in myself the streak of flippant gloss that had ended up with my exposure to such things as Sophy Brent: my more than exposure, my positive attraction towards. Was it some superficiality in myself, or some obsequious provincial desire for fastness and smartness that had got me where I was? I looked back at the people I had liked and the things I had done, and the earliest memory I could find that seemed relevant was from a classroom at my first school in Cambridge, when I was, I should imagine, eleven years old. As homework we had been told to learn Tennyson's *Break, break, break*, and in class we all had to get up, one by one, and recite the thing.

I had liked the poem, I had learned it with enthusiasm, I thought it was most touching and poetic. But the frightful thing was that so apparently did everyone else. I can remember most distinctly the expressions of sanctimonious sorrow and world-weariness on the faces of little girls whose judgement I usually thought atrocious. " 'I would that my heart could utter,' " they said, " 'the thoughts that arise in me,' " and I said to myself then and there that unless I could utter the thoughts that arouse in me I would try to keep my mouth shut rather than make such an exhibition of myself. What annoyed me most of all was the way they all started off, so reverentially, saying, " 'Break, break, break,' by Alfred Lord Tennyson," just as it was printed in Palgrave's *The Golden Treasury*, as though to omit one syllable of that "Alfred Lord" would somehow detract from the poem's magical incantation.

This is the first instance I can remember of my own revulsion from what I most liked, and my first desire to give it a good kick in the teeth for the sake of human independence. It was all very well for Alfred Lord Tennyson to say *Oh well for the fisherman's boy*, but whose fault was it but my own if I could not find it in my life to say *Oh well for Emma Evans?* Poetry is one thing and living another, I said to myself at the age of eleven, and I steered clear of poetry for the sake, or so I thought, of the other thing.

7

AFTER that Sophy Brent came to visit me nearly
every day. She irritated me unbearably most of
the time: she smoked incessantly and never
used an ashtray; she followed me into the kitch-
en while I made tea or coffee or supper and
helped herself to the children's orange juice;
she made a great hit with Flora, who would
hang around her for hours and refer to her
lovingly as "Sofa"; and she was always talking
about David and asking me where he was. I
could not decide why she chose my company,
although I realized that nobody else paid her
very much attention. She was very unfortunately placed, at the age of nineteen, in that
she was straight out of drama school and in
this, her second job, she was required to play a
leading part in a company of fairly distinguished and experienced actors. They would
not have liked her much even if she had been
good, and as from all accounts she was not
good they took every opportunity to run her
down. I think she thought that I was the only
person around who was both disconnected
from the theatre and tolerably smart: to associate with me was not, at any rate, to step down
the scale. And for my part, although I was ir-

ritated by her I did not dislike her: there was
something genuinely disarming in her effusive-
ness, and she had such physical charm that
with me she could get away with anything.
She was nice to have round, like flowers or a
bowl of fruit. And I did not find her childish, as
the others claimed to find her: I saw in her
the beginnings of some rare high verbal duplicity. There was nothing wrong with her, I
maternally thought, that time would not put
right. It annoyed me that I should see so much
of her, but she was not the first silly girl that
I had seen much of.

I would have been even less annoyed had I
had more to do. As the first night drew nearer,
David and everyone else grew busier and my
life became a barren waste. The weather was
shocking: it rained every day, and it was impossible even to go for boring walks. Flora was
my joy and my delight, but so alien to me
were the feelings with which she inspired me
that I managed to unite intense joy and intense boredom in the same instant, and the
pain of the rift made me even worse. The final
grievance was that David, when he was at
home, was intensely disagreeable: he is always
affected by the part he is playing, but in television a part only lasts for three weeks, whereas this time I was condemned to a whole season
of Flamineo who happened to be a self-centered existentialist pimp. Apart from the nature
of the character, I think David was also intensely worried about whether he was going to be a
success or not. He cared tremendously about
what Wyndham Farrar thought of him, and
was very anxious that everyone should take him

seriously as a proper straight actor. I saw no reason to doubt that he would be so taken, myself, but he is not possessed with great self-assurance.

The week before the opening night he suggested that I should go along and see the first technical run-through of *The White Devil*. As the alternative was *Sunday Night at the London Palladium* with Pascal, I said that I would go, and I made my way to the theatre through the pouring rain at about eight in the evening. David said that he had asked permission from Wyndham for me to watch. It was an added interest to know that I was in some measure expected, and I was therefore in some measure expectant. I sat at the back of the auditorium to watch: it was dark there, and I could only just make out the forms of the other actors, technicians and hangers-on who were dotted sparsely around the stalls. I located Sophy quickly, from her continuous giggle. Wyndham Farrar was walking up and down one of the aisles, and David was on stage. I like watching rehearsals: they are far more interesting than performances. One can see in a rehearsal every detail of what has preceded: who loves whom, who is nervous, who is confident, who is vain, who has been bullied by the director, who is admired by the rest of the cast, who is on the verge of tearful disaster. A performance does not wholly conceal such things, but it conceals some of them; whereas here before me lay the whole pattern, or what I liked to think was the whole pattern. There was, too, a wonderful counterpoise between the life of the play itself and the life and dialogue that the actors would

assume in the incessant breaks for lighting
cues, music cues, furniture rearrangements
and so forth, which were, rather than any more
artistic concern, the purpose of the occasion.
Peter Yates would break off at a line like *Thou
hast led me like a heathen sacrifice, With gar-
lands and with fatal yokes of flowers, To mine
eternal ruin* in order to move a cushion on the
bed, to complain about his boots or to put his
arm round Viola, the waiting woman, and whisper in her ear, so that the notions of over-
polished boots and eternal ruins mingled
strangely.

Natalie Winter, who was playing Vittoria
Corombona, the distinguished courtesan, was
as cool and professional as ever. She spoke little
and did perfectly what was required of her,
giving a perfect small reproduction of what her
eventual performance was to be. She seemed
worried, however, about her appearance: at
every pause she sat down quietly on the bed,
while the others joked and laughed and complained and sucked peppermints, to pull fret-
fully at the neckline of her tight boned bodice.
She was not really an attractive woman at all,
though she dressed up well: her body, all built
up and hard inside the boned gown, looked
wonderful, but her wig had not as yet arrived,
and her thin neck and face and wispy hair rose
out of the low velvet boundaries in school-
mistressly incongruity. Peter Yates was looking
splendid in the usual stage style of boots and
open white shirts, and David was of course
wandering around in his own clothes. He has
never liked the idea of dressing up, I will say
that much for him.

They were making interminably slow progress. Between eight and nine they went over the
same scene change and the ensuing scene about
fifteen times. Everyone but Natalie seemed on
the verge of revolt. The difficulty was purely
technical: it was a question of synchronizing
the appearance of a bed and a few bits of
scenery with the arrival of a group of actors.
There was much talk about cue lights and other
things, and finally Wyndham, whose voice I
had hardly heard, said:

"Well, you can pack up for ten minutes while
I work this one out."

And they all went off to the green room,
while Wyndham walked up and down the
aisle smoking. On his tenth return he stopped at
the end of the row where I was sitting and said:

"That's Mrs. Evans, isn't it?"

"Yes," I said.

"I'll sit down for a moment," he said, and he
sat down, leaving one vacant seat between
us, over which he leaned to offer me a cigarette. I accepted because I wanted him to
light it for me.

"Well," he said as he put out his lighter,
"there's not very much to see here tonight, is
there?"

"Oh, I don't know," I said. "There seems to be
quiet a lot going on, in one way and another."

"You think so?"

"Yes, I think so."

"Are you finding Hereford any more interesting than you were when I last spoke to you? I
haven't forgotten what you said."

"You haven't time for what I said. You're a

very busy man," I said. "What are you going to do about that scene change?"

"Oh, that. That's perfectly straightforward. They'll all get it right first time when they get back, they were just not concentrating. They always say things are impossible, they panic."

"So you're not thinking about it at all?"

"Why should I? I know what I want."

"Do you?"

"On the whole. Yes. On the whole, I think that I do. It's usually quite straightforward. If other people don't panic."

"It's a good play," I said.

"Yes, it is, isn't it? I think so. They don't think so. They all like doing it because they all think they've got the best part, though your husband is the only one who's right about thinking it, but they don't think much of the play. They think it's a load of rubbish."

And he sat there for a moment more in the semidarkness, and although I knew it was impossible that he should sit down in this way for no purpose, and impossible that he should make these remarks to anyone just for the sake of the remarks, there was still enough doubt to make me sit hard and clenched and frightened, just in case this was one of those tiny, unexplained loopholes in human behaviour, just in case he was not going in the direction in which I knew that he was going. And doubt being the essence of excitement, I was excited and happy as I sat there. He got up and went a moment afterwards, saying no more, and the rehearsal continued.

At one o'clock in the morning I was still sitting there, and the action of the play had pro-

gressed by two acts. I had gathered that Viola
White, who was playing Zanche, the black ser-
vant, was on the verge of an affair with Neville;
that big kind Michael was after thin sad Julian,
who did not like to oblige or to disoblige; and
that David was going to be very good.

He is sometimes extraordinarily good. I was
also more impressed by the play than I had expected to be: it still seemed an odd choice for a
festive season, but it had far more real strength
and coherence than I had hoped for. I wondered how much of the clear shape and intention were due to Wyndham Farrar, and I hoped
much of them, but I am not one of those who
can decipher with ease where an actor or a
designer or a director has gone locally and
specifically right or wrong, at the expense of or to
the benefit of the others concerned.

At a quarter past one I thought it was time
that I should be getting home. I was afraid that
Joe might have woken or that the house might
have burned down. And I was tired: Joe still
woke me at six every morning. So I put my
cigarettes and matches and litter back into my
handbag, tied on my head-square, put on my
damp raincoat and set off down the corridor
towards the pass door that connected back-
stage with the auditorium. The front of the
house was locked, and I would have to go out
through the stage door. I had just put my hand
on the pass doorknob when the corridor light
went out. I pushed the door open, and saw
nothing on the other side but blackness, and
heard the cries of delight and annoyance and
amazement that indicated a total fuse. I stood
quite still where I was, waiting for someone to

switch something on, but the darkness continued as the noise increased. People started to
yell for electricians, for Wyndham Farrar, for
matches. I stood and listened and smelled the
dust and varnish and sawdust and size and all
the fake smells of the theatre. I dared not
move for fear of getting in the way. People were
groping about in all directions, some of them
clearly profiting from the dramatic blackout
to achieve in five minutes what they might not
otherwise have got round to for days. It was
that time of night when anxiety and exhaustion lead to all kinds of compensatory contact.
In the distant gleam of a match I saw David
with one arm round Sophy and the other round
a girl called Mavis, and then the light flickered
and went out. Quite near me someone started
to go into a long explanation, which he shouted
at the top of his voice to someone else in the
auditorium, about what was wrong with the
emergency supply. I thought I would retreat,
and I stepped back through the door into the
corridor, which was so dark that I could not see
my own hand when I held it up before me.
It was not like the darkness in one's own house:
the thick carpet was unfamiliar, I could not lo-
cate the walls, I was unwilling to lose myself in
the maze of corridors, foyers and staircases
that extended backwards behind me. So I
waited, with everyone else, for magic light to
be restored, but before anything else happened
I heard footsteps coming toward me along
the corridor, gropingly. Quickly I searched
for my matches and started to light myself a
cigarette, for the thought of someone banging
into me namelessly filled me with alarm. At the

sight of the flame the footsteps quickened, and
with embarrassed courtesy I extended the
match into the darkness, and as it burned low
to my finger ends Wyndham himself closed up
on me. I had just time to see his face before
I had to blow out the light. He was duskily
gilded and heavily furrowed with more years
than I was accustomed to: forty-three of them,
to be exact, and why not be exact? The dimness
and the suddenly extinguished brightness and
the ensuing undefined closeness reminded me of
something, and my guts sagged or stiffened or
dropped, I am not sure what they do, but they
do it from intense fear or apprehension or
memory. We stood there in silence together,
and I wondered if perhaps it had been too dark
for him to see my face. But he said after a
short pause:

"Emma Evans, that's you, isn't it?"

"Yes, it's me," I said.

"I thought you would have gone by now."

"I was just going when it happened."

"Extraordinary. This kind of thing is always
happening to me. Fuses, fires, disasters. The
last show I was working on a weight fell from
the flies and missed me by six inches. It went
right through the stage and hit a man in the
wardrobe. It just shows you, there's a providence in the fall of a sparrow. Don't you believe that?"

"Yes, I do believe it," I said, whispering in
response to his whisper.

"Wait a minute," he said, "I've got a light
somewhere," and he pulled out the lighter with
which he had earlier lit my cigarette. By its
petrol flame I could once more see his face,

somewhat old and blue this time, without the
yellow warmth that my match had lent him.
He stared at me and I stared back. I noticed
that he was carrying a whisky bottle and a
cardboard beaker in one hand, holding the bottle militantly by the neck, with the beaker attached by one finger.

"Well, well," he said, "Emma Evans. How
extraordinary. I knew there was somebody at
the end of the corridor, but I didn't think it was
going to be you. What did you find of such interest here to keep you so long?"

"I like watching," I said.

"Do you? You don't look all that passive to
me."

"Appearances are misleading," I said.

He did not reply, but continued to stare
at me, holding his lighter up towards my face
with a mixture of intimacy and stagey distance that I found embarrassing.

"Don't you think," I said, trying to shift
out of the direct small limelight, "that you
ought to go and do something about this fuse of
yours? They don't seem to have built this theatre very well if the lights go the very first time
you try to use them."

"You're always trying to get me to do things,"
he said with some exaggeration. "I don't know
anything about fuses, it's got nothing to do
with me at all. That's not my province, fuses. I
remember now, one of the nastiest evenings of
my life was to do with a fuse box. I was with
this girl in a flat in Paddington, just after the
war it was, and there was some kind of crisis
going on, her career, or my career, or something like that, and we were just getting

through to the other side when all the light went out on us. She was running an electric fire and a toaster off the light switch. Anyway, like a flash she got out a screwdriver from somewhere or other and told me to go out in the hall and find the fuse box and mend it, so off I went, out into the hall and straight down the stairs and out into the street and home. I've never seen her since; she did quite well in America, I think. I've still got that screwdriver, I was really crazy about that girl. I'd have done anything for her, anything I could do, but what she wanted was always the impossible: fuse boxes, to look like Marlene Dietrich, all that kind of thing. It's a long time since I thought about her. And then you say you don't believe in providence."

"I didn't say that," I said. "I believe in providence. And in coincidence."

"Do you really? So do I. It's one or the other, for instance, that you should be telling me to go off and mend that fuse. Women don't understand how complicated fuses are."

"I can do them myself," I said. "They're quite easy, once you know."

"I bet you couldn't deal with one this size," he said. "It's probably a national electricity cut, and nothing to do with me at all."

"Not at this time of night, surely."

"Why not? A very sensible time to have a power cut, I'd have thought. I wonder how much all this is costing us in overtime."

"You'd better go and find out," I said. "You're wasting your lighter fuel."

"Yes, I am. I was thinking, Mrs. Evans, perhaps it might be a good idea if I took you out to dinner. Sometime when your husband is working. You must be left alone a lot. I was going to ask you next week, when these plays have opened, but since you're here I'll ask you now. Next Wednesday they'll all be busy running through *The Clandestine Marriage*. What about next Wednesday?"

"Out to dinner?"

"Yes, out to dinner. What's wrong with that? Don't you eat?"

"Oh yes. I eat."

"Next Wednesday then."

"Surely you ought to be keeping an eye on *The Clandestine Marriage*, oughtn't you? With so little time to go."

"Is it a permanent trait in your character, this desire to tell other people their duty? Or do you just do it to me?"

"All right then, next Wednesday."

"I'll pick you up at your house. Is that convenient? We can go somewhere in the car. Do you like cars?"

"Yes. I like cars."

He looked at me thoughtfully, and I as steadily regarded him. I think we were both very happy at that moment, for we were both regarding, with a little awe, the unpredictable. Then he said:

"Do you want to go now? I'll let you out through the front door if you like, and then we won't get mixed up with all those people."

And he led me back along the corridor, through the dark deserted foyer to the glass doors of the main entrance, and just as he put his key in the lock the lights all went on again. We blinked at each other in that bright and empty festive place. I was a little stunned: he looked older, more formidable in the light.

"Perhaps you could tell David," I said as I paused on the threshold, "that I've gone home."

"I'll tell him," said Wyndham, and I walked off into the rain.

On the way home I began to wonder if I had not been extremely silly: my sense of muted triumph and exhilaration gave way to an anxiety that at first formulated itself in terms of the doubtful wisdom of going out with another man alone. It was a fact that since my marriage I had been out with nobody but the most harmless friends of my childhood: I had not had time. There would have been no point in saying no, and yet I felt that I had involved myself in disaster by saying yes. It was not merely that our appointment had a distinct flavour of the clandestine, nor that Wyndham Farrar himself seemed to be a dangerous undertaking, though both these factors were involved. It was more that the way I had said yes, the helpless, rash, needing way I had been unable to refuse, laid me open to all sorts of conjectures about myself and my position. I thought of David, and Flora, and Joseph, and myself, and with each step I realized more clearly that for the last few months, for the last year, I personally, I myself, the part of me that was not a function and a smile and a mother, had been curled up and rotten with grief and patience and pain. I walked quicker and quicker as myself stretched and put out damp, bony wings. I hated myself. I did not want to give myself a chance, I would rather have said no to that invitation and concentrated on my Liverpool teapots and my even temper.

When I got home I could not get to sleep: the enormity of my hope seemed to me the measure of the enormity of my failure and disappointment, and I did not wish to feel sorry for myself, I did not wish to have failed. I lay there and wondered what frightful depths of need the chance words of a man whom I did not know and had no reason to like had revealed in me; and I saw then clearly what later became confused, that I was about to be chained, in a fashion so arbitrary that it frightened me, to a passion so accidental that it confirmed nothing but my own inadequacy and inability to grow. As a child I used to comfort myself by saying, "I am a child, this will pass." But I was no longer a child, there was no reason why this kind of blind rashness should ever pass. This was me, this was myself, this hungry bony bird who was ready for some unexplained famine to eat straw and twigs and paper.

I had just got to sleep when David got in. He woke me up to ask me what I thought of everything and everyone, and then he wanted me to hear his lines. I refused crossly; but what I felt was worse than crossness, it was total, total separation. They had told me it would fail, and I saw, suddenly, what they had meant.

8

I woke in the morning with a hangover: I had had three hours' sleep, and as I stumbled out of bed to pick up hungry Joseph and give him the one feed a day which he was not yet taking from a bottle, I felt the weary debt for such a little flutter of vanity, for so mild an excursion onto forbidden ground. I looked down at my baby's cheerful sucking face, and I smiled mechanically, and he dropped the nipple to smile back, and I thought, You fool, if you knew how little I meant to smile at you. The next few days I spent in a grey and yellow fog: nothing could waken me, I walked around as though I were asleep, with my head heavy and my arms hanging as though they were too great a weight for me to carry around with me. Looking back, it seems amazing that I should for so little reason have felt so much: such lifelessness, such long hours, such a fear of waking up, such boredom. I had felt bored before, but only occupationally. Now I felt bored with my life. I look back on that week, and on the first time I went out with Wyndham, with amazement: so much passion, it now seems, and so little cause. When I was a girl such an encounter, such an episode, would have meant nothing to me, I would have taken it in my stride, with gusto, with tears and enjoyment. But now, after more than three years of forbearance and patience, and after a strong diet of David, which must have in some way enlarged my capacity for serious emotion, I felt both far more and far less. I felt far more desire, with far less hope.

I look back on that first outing, and it has a strange pickled charm, like a fly in amber, or a sour black walnut, or a dead brown rose that I once saw trapped in a block of cut glass in an antique shop in Venice. Wyndham did not call for me at my house: he thought better of it, and picked me up at an anonymous meeting point by a post office. I liked his car: it was a maroon Jaguar, and it seemed to be made inside of solid polished wood. He took me to a restaurant somewhere in Wales. I had never in my life been in Wales before, and it was a satisfactory slap in the eye for David, to be there without him. We drank a lot and stared at each other over the food, and he told me many stories about his life: he told me about women, all sorts of women, and I liked him for the way that he seemed to have been ready to have a go at anything. His stories all had a hit-and-miss nature, and the naïve and ready way that he rushed into them, willing to capture my attention by any extravagance, reminded me of myself in those days when I would tell perfect strangers that my mother was dying, simply in order to compel their attention. And he compelled mine, for it was not a sense of pathos that he aroused, but rather an unwilling admiration for his perpetual readiness.

I myself was far from ready: for so long I had been effacing myself from any serious sexual attention that I had almost lost the knack. I am not saying that I am one of these women who when married lose all interest in their appearance and in the admiration of others. On the contrary, my appearance has always obsessed me, but there is a difference bteween desiring to attract attention in the street or at a first night and being able to sustain it through an evening à deux. I did not dare at first to take the risk. I hedged, I did not have the courage to follow up my excursions nor the self-absorption to maintain, once struck, a fine attitude of arm or head or eye. But gradually I began to feel the old pulls and pressures. And I found that I was not bad at it at all: I knew that I looked imposing, and eventually my conversation began to regain a little of the wideness and sharpness that I had for years been attempting to soften and enclose. I told my stories, too, and not this time, if I remember rightly, about my mother. He was not the kind of man to shy away from provocation.

Indeed, the amount of provocation that went on was quite exhausting. When we finally ended our meal and went back to the car, we fell into each other's arms on the front seat with an avid apprehension that even in retrospect retains its intensity. We withdrew quickly enough, with the usual mutterings, gazing and hair-straightening.

"Come on, let's go," I said as I buttoned up my coat. "I must get back."

For although it was impossible for David to be back before midnight I still feared the unforeseen. So we set off back again. It seemed too late to retreat and too early to be committed. I was hazy and drunk and tired, and the big car moved along with a quiet powerful airiness. I felt suspended, cushioned, inactive; and after a while I said:

"Oh God, this is really rather frightful, have we really got to go through with all this?" and instead of asking me what I meant he said:

"Yes, I think we should, don't you? Cheer up, it's never as bad as you think it's going to be, there are always a few consolations, you know."

"There weren't many last time," I said.

"Who was last time?"

"David was last time."

"Really? Nobody since David?"

"I haven't had any time since David," I said. "He's kept me very busy. I haven't had a night off in years."

"I don't believe you. The first time I set eyes on you, I said, That's a dangerous-looking woman."

"The first time you set eyes on me I was pregnant."

"Excluding that occasion. I don't count that."

"Well, I'm glad to know I don't look as harmless as I am."

"What would David say if he knew where you were? You haven't by any chance told him, have you?"

"Of course I haven't told him. I wasn't going to spoil my chances before I knew what my chances were. Our relationship isn't all that sophisticated, you know."

"I'm glad you didn't tell him. I wouldn't like

David Evans staring at me. I wouldn't like to
get hit by David Evans. Welshmen are a rotten
pugnacious lot, you know."

"I know."

"Does he beat you up?"

"Do you mind?" I said crossly, shifting farther away in my seat. "I'm not all that bloody
feeble myself, you know."

And after that we drove back in silence until,
just before we reached the town, I suddenly
and without premeditation said:

"Don't worry, I'm really very happy here,
you know," and he released the gear lever and
took my hand: he was at that moment turning a
corner, at a speed quite concealed by the nature of the car's motion, and as we went
round in the narrow country road we overtook
an apparently stationary van, passing it silently with a few inches to spare. He had not
counted on it, we had very nearly had an accident and yet the speed and silence with
which it had happened made it seem an hallu-
cination. His grasp on my hand tightened very
slightly, and that was the only concession we
made to what might have been some kind of
end.

I got to bed just after one. We had agreed
to meet the next week, after the opening of the
first two plays, in the lull before rehearsals for
the last play of the season began.

"Think about me," he said as we parted.

"I'll think about you," I said. "I think about
most things, I won't miss you out."

I took David's copy of *Who's Who in the
Theatre* to bed with me, and guiltily, like a
schoolgirl looking up ominous, suggestive

words in the dictionary, I looked him up:
Wyndham Farrar, it said, *director, born Grantham, s. of Percy Edward Farrar, F.R.C.S., and
Laura Montefiore, e.* Oundle and Royal Acade-
my of Dramatic Art, served in the Middle
East during the war and worked in Far East for
ENSA, 45-7, subsequently worked in rep at
here and there; and then there followed a list
of his successes in this country and in America.
He had directed three television plays and two
experimental films, apart from his stage work,
and had written a book called *The Art of
Transience,* published 1952. His recreations
were listed as travelling and cricket, and his
address was an address in Wimple Street. I
had known about his career, enough at least to
know that the otherwise impressive book he
had written was largely a collection of his dramatic journalism. What really caught my attention was that *born Grantham, s. of Percy
Edward Farrar. F.R.C.S., and Laura Montefiore,* for these words seemed to contain the key
to some mystery. I did not know why, but they
seemed to explain what he was doing in Hereford, and his whole nonchalant attitude to a
profession that most pursue with burning,
never resting zeal.

When I had finished with the book, I got out
of bed and returned it to its place on the shelf:
I did not want David to know that I had been
consulting it, I felt that he would know the
exact references that I had required. I had embarked upon deceit. David woke me an hour
later when he came in, at half past two, and
started to tell me about what Selwyn had said
to him about his performance. I told him to

shut up and get out of my bed and go and
sleep on the sofa, and that if I didn't get a
decent night's sleep I'd go back to London in
the morning. He said he bloody well wished I
would, and we fell asleep side by side. I think
that was the first time that he did not know
and could not have known, having no access
to it, the real reason for my anger.

9

THE next day I took the children to the park. I
wandered ghostlike behind the pram, glad
that I had its bar to lean on. Flora went on
the swings, and wept bitterly when it was time
to come off, as I had known she would, and I
wondered why she was always so blindly eager
to get on when she knew what tears would be
entailed in the ending of it. And I wondered,
too, how I could even consider Wyndham
Farrar: it hardly seemed worth the trouble. I
watched Flora's screwed, woeful face, and I
thought, Shall I never, never learn? Other people
learn. Other people keep away from the swings
and the roundabouts.

I hardly saw David in the last day or two
before the opening. The *Clandestine Marriage*
was to open on the Tuesday, and *The White
Devil* on the following Friday. The proxim-

ity of the dates was causing much avoidable
overwork, late night panic and confusion which
everyone involved seemed to need and to enjoy. Various celebrities were due to arrive for
the opening night, including an important
duchess and Mrs. Von Blerke, the backer. I had
nothing to do but to work out what I should
wear, having already organized myself an es-
cort, who was at once a *coup* and a mistake: he
was a novelist whom I had known for some
years, an American who was currently working
as drama critic for the magazine of which I
had once graced the cover. He was both in-
telligent and important, but on the other hand,
there are drawbacks in sitting next to critics on
first nights, at least when one's husband is ap-
pearing.

On the morning of the day itself I went out
to buy a card with jokes, rabbits, or daisies on
to send to Sophy: it was her big day, her first
big part, and I felt that I could not grudge her
a card of good wishes in view of all the coffee,
tea and black currant juice of mine that she
had drunk over the past few weeks. On the
way I passed a shop that I had never noticed
before: it said FARRAR: CREMATION EM-
BALMING INTERMENT. Oh well, I thought
as I registered the jolt it gave me, what silly significance life is made of. And at the news
agent's where I had gone to select my card
the headlines of all the papers, spread out *en
masse*, were devoted to some horrific air disaster over the Atlantic: more than a hundred
missing, feared drowned, with twenty-six mirac-
ulously rescued. I had not looked at our paper
that morning, and anyway, we take *The Times*.

I bought a copy of *The Guardian* to see if there were any reports of what the survivors had said: it is interesting to know what people think who unexpectedly survive death, whether it seems to them to be coincidence or providence. There were no spectacular remarks this time, but it said that the only child on board, a three-year-old boy, had been rescued, and that it was believed that his mother had not been on the plane, that he had been flying to join her in England. And at this fact, this small fact, I felt my eyes fill with tears of gratitude. I stood there crying in the news agent's because he would not have to say endlessly "Where's Mummy?" with no answer, whereas for all I knew, for all the paper said, he had never set eyes on her in his life since birth, she might well have deserted him in the cradle. I thought of Flora or Joe, wet with all those oceans of water, and I cried. Then I bought a card for Sophy, with blue rabbits, and went back home. When I got back, David was still in bed. He called to me as he heard me on the stairs, and I went to him.

"There was someone on the phone for you," he said.

"Oh. Who?"

"I don't know, he didn't say. Some man."

"It must have been Mike."

"I know Mike. It wasn't Mike."

"Oh. Then I can't think who it can have been."

"What's the matter with you?"

"Nothing. Look." I gave him the paper, with the account of the air disaster.

"What about it?" he said. "We heard all

about that at rehearsal last night. What's so special about that? You didn't know anyone on it, did you?"

"No."

"Then what's the matter?"

"Nothing. It's just so accidental. So arbitrary."

"Accidents always are accidental."

"There was a little boy."

"Oh, for Christ's sake. Kids are being massacred all over the place every day, in all sorts of ways."

"Very funny."

"Don't be so bloody stupid."

"Bloody stupid yourself. Selfish great oaf," I said, and left the room, with no profound increase in dignity or sentiment.

An hour later a telegram arrived for me. By pure chance I got to the door first and managed to read it before anyone else saw that it had arrived. It said PLEASE RING FLAT TWELVE THIRTY, FARRAR. I put it in my pocket, and David called from his room:

"Who was that at the door?"

My mind was as blank as paper. I pretended not to have heard. He called again, and I went into the kitchen. Silence was the most convincing conduct I could assume. And for the next hour I tried to think of some way of leaving the house at the precise hour at which I always do the children's lunch, in order to go to the phone box on the corner. How simple and how impossible it would be to walk out and do it can hardly be imagined by anyone used to living alone. I peeled the potatoes and invented many elaborate excuses to myself, all of which seemed out of the question; and yet it seemed equally out of the question to be defeated at this, the first and simplest innocent step. How on earth could anyone even contemplate a concealed affair, or even a concealed emotion, without being able to leave the house for five minutes?

At twenty-five past twelve I left the lunch cooking on the stove, asked Flora if she would like to go for a little walk, told Pascal to keep an eye on Joe and set off down the stairs. I made no excuse at all: I walked out and I was trembling like a leaf. When I got to the phone box, Flora insisted on putting the pennies in, and then sat on the floor and started to read the directory. Wyndham answered almost immediately.

"This is Emma," I said.

"Emma. Thank God you rang. I tried to get you on the phone, but I only got that husband of yours."

"Yes, I know."

"Did he know it was me?"

"No. I worked it out. What's the matter?"

"The most frightful farce imaginable. Too ghastly for words. You know the woman who gave all the money for this place, that crackpot who thinks she's some descendant of Garrick?"

"Mrs. Von Blerke."

"You do know about her. She was on that plane that went down in the Atlantic last night."

"You're not serious."

"Of course I'm serious."

"Is she dead then?"

"I wish to God I knew. I've been trying to find out since eleven o'clock last night. I can't think what to try next; nobody seems to have a list of survivors, nobody seems to know where anyone is. She's one chance in five of having survived, and if she has she's bobbing up and down somewhere in a small boat in the middle of the ocean. What the hell am I supposed to do about it, do you imagine?"

"What can you do?"

"She's got to be here. What's going to happen to all the ribbon-snipping and champagne and seating arrangements? I'm going out of my mind. Poor bloody woman. If she is dead, do you think anyone would be crazy enough to expect us to postpone the whole show? I hardly know whether I'd be crazy enough to expect it myself. This is the kind of decision I keep clear of, but there's no one else to make it."

"Poor Wyndham."

"Do you think she'll arrive at the curtain, dripping and ghastly? One in five isn't hopeless as odds, you know."

"How old was she?"

"Sixty. Sixty something. Poor bloody woman, she was such a nice old thing, she was so looking forward to meeting Her Grace. What a frightful way to pack it in."

"I've never known anyone who had an accident before."

"Haven't you? I have. But this is the first time one has happened to me."

"I can't do anything to help you, though, Wyndham."

"I know you can't. I just wanted to tell you. I thought you might be interested. Seems to be a perfect example of something or other, if you know what I mean. Me here worrying about a handful of people out of *Who's Who* and her floundering away there."

"How many people know about it?"

"Only the people who knew which plane she was on. The management, Selwyn. None of the company, as far as I know."

"Couldn't you just say that she had to post-pone her visit?"

"I suppose so. I suppose so. Shall I be seeing you tonight? Are you coming tonight, or are you such a grand wife that you don't bother to turn up?"

"I'll be coming. I'm not as grand as all that."

"Not quite. Would you like me to send you some flowers? A corsage, as they say? I'm send-ing one to everyone else under the sun, I might as well send you one as well. With a false *billet-doux*, from your loving uncle? Would you like that?"

"Not at all. It would be highly inappro-priate."

"What a shame. It would have given me something useful to do, ringing the florist again. I'm sending Natalie Winter an azalea this time, in a large pot. The last show of mine that she was in I sent her a bunch of some quite unlikely big flowers, orange they were, and she arrived at the party afterwards with at least half of them pinned on her dress. Her dress was cerise silk. At least she can't pin on an azalea. I'd bet-ter send Mrs. Von Blerke a wreath. Do you think Interflora deliver to Boston?"

"Wyndham, I've got to go."

"What for?"

"Lunch."

"Oh, that's all right. I'll be seeing you. Have a nice lunch. Thanks for ringing."

Flora did not want to leave the telephone directory: she was busy tearing out pages. All the way back to the house she yelled, "Book, book," and I was glad that she could say no more. When I got back David said:

"Where have you been?" and I said that I had been to the post.

"Book," said Flora.

"She means letter," I said as I tied her bib on and sat her down at the table. "She wanted to put the letter in the box, and I put it in without thinking, so now she's cross."

"She's always cross," said David, and started to play this little piggy with her fingers. She was overcome with delight, she thinks David is the most amusing person in the world.

In the afternoon David went out to rehearse curtain calls, and I sat and thought about Mrs. Von Blerke and death by water and played with Flora and wondered how to wear my hair for the evening. At five Mike Papini arrived, full of indignation about the train journey.

"They told me it was just by Oxford," he said miserably, as we drank our tea. "I'll never get back again. Lucky you asked me to stay the night. What a place to get to. What do they mean by opening a theatre here?"

"Not everyone lives in London," I said, watching Mike with the astonishment which he always causes in me: he is so very tall and thin and American, and every bone and angle of him is full of absurd sensitivity, sensitivity car-

ried to a painful, ridiculous degree. The back
of his neck has the frightful tenderness of a
child's, and the shortness of his hair imposes it
upon the view. I have known Mike for years: I
first met him in Rome, when he was a typical
American boy abroad and I was a typical English schoolgirl abroad, and I lost touch with
him for some time after that, apart from a des-
ultory plangent letter or two, until he turned
up again in London, a literary success and
working on the magazine with which I myself
had odd connections. I did not exactly like
him: in some ways he was rather unpleasant,
being a perfect case of a man so interested in
his own reactions that he cannot appreciate action or quality at all, and I remember one
event, when a girl friend of his committed suicide, that almost put me off him for life. I was
so much less interested in him than in whatever the wretched girl had been wanting, but
all I ever learned from him was the tortuous
succession of pettinesses that she had caused
him to endure. However, he interested me: he
always had something to say, even if it was
only the usual complaint about journalism sti-
fling his soul. And also I must admit that since
he had actually had two novels printed, and
moderately good firsthand ones at that, my respect for his sensitivities had increased. It was
interesting to have him there, telling me about
London, and who wrote what about whom in
what, and who had had a five-poem spread in
Encounter, and who had gone off to teach crea-
tive writing in which university in the States.
I lapped all this up, starved as I was for casual
gossip and deprived as I was amongst so many

theatricals of any literary chat at all. So I listened with far more attention and enthusiasm
than I usually gave him, and when the time
came to dress he continued his conversation
through the closed bedroom door. I was struck
principally by his morbid concern lest his own
responses should harden, which seemed to be
far from likely, for he was as bare and as reed-
in-the-wind as ever, and by his lack of generosity about his colleagues, whom he treated with
an asperity that few actors could match. He
had nothing of the superficial goodwill and interest and keenness and apparent love that is
so widespread amongst actors that I sometimes
think it must be not superficial but profound.
He was like a Cambridge discussion, after
weeks of messy latitude: not a darling from
him, not a kiss on the cheek or an arm around
the shoulders.

And yet as the evening progressed, I began
to have my doubts. When we arrived at the
theatre, surrounded by yards of new green
plush, glass doors and dimly remembered faces,
he had already indicated that he thought I was
wasting my time in Hereford, which was the
kind of extrovert personal suggestion that he
would never have risked without some reason
of his own. I became rather annoyed with him,
as he tried to continue talking in his usual intense vein about whether or not it was permissible to keep on writing the same novel over
and over again with different characters,
when all I wanted to do was to have a good
look round and spot who was there and to try
and work out from the atmosphere whether
Mrs. Von Blerke was dead or alive. It was im-

possible to tell. There was no black crepe, no slip in the programme, no air of doom; but on the other hand, she did not appear to be there. We took our places in the auditorium, and a couple of minutes before the curtain went up I saw Wyndham arrive and take his place just in front of us, in the second row of the dress circle. He was accompanied by a smart, thin, middle-aged woman and her husband, both of whom I felt I had seen before, though I could not think where. He noticed me and said good evening. As luck, of course, would have it, he was sitting almost directly in front of me, only two seats away, so that I could hear everything he said, and had the impression that he could hear me. His nearness disturbed me: faint physical aching started up inside, and I leaned back sick with indignation and folded my hands on my stomach, where they could feel almost as much disturbance as they had become accustomed to feel from a more independent inner life. I hated this conception as much as I hated the others, and this time I had no hope even of eventual birth.

When the curtain went up, I stopped thinking about Wyndham and Mike Papini and started to worry about David and whether he might turn out to be frightful. It was some time since I had seen him in action. He was not frightful: he was very good, and the best thing in it, so that cheered me. The production was mediocre and pageantlike, all fancy dress and robust comic business, but the audience loved it. The only disaster was poor Sophy, who was playing the lead, the clandestine bride herself. She was really bad: she looked enchanting, but she spoke in the most wonderful stilted twentieth-century way imaginable. The art of timing eluded her completely: she dropped other people's lines with malicious innocence and mistimed her own in the same reckless way. Garrick's sentences, like most eighteenth-century sentences, tend to be long, and Sophy had so little grasp of syntax that she never appeared to have foreseen the end at the beginning. Even a simple sentence like *You see, Mr. Lovewell, the effects of indiscretion* was too much for her, and she managed to break it up three times. It was painful to watch her: she was like a good tennis club player who had wandered into Wimbledon. Every time she opened her mouth, for the first three quarters of an hour, Mike muttered "Oh Gawd" and scribbled a note on his programme; and he was about as insensitive to the spoken English dramatic tongue as anyone of his profession could be.

During the interval I saw and briefly spoke to Mr. and Mrs. Scott, who said that they had heard Mary had been to see me and that she and her husband were not there as they were not too much of theatregoers, managing to imply in one breath that they themselves were right to go to first nights, that their daughter and her husband were right to stay away and that I was wrong to be there with a man whom they did not recognize and whom I did not introduce. Mike and I both had a double gin, and on the way back to our seats, as he propelled me through the crush at the second bell, he took hold of my elbow with his large bony fist, clasping it so tightly that he hurt. I was still standing and arranging the folds of my dress when Wyndham, returning to his seat, brushed past me; his dinner-jacketed arm touched my bare arm, and he turned and smiled and said:

"Sorry, Emma. Enjoying yourself?"

"Naturally," I said, and the lights went down.

I could no longer concentrate on the play during the second act: I sat in my own dark knot and thought. About Mrs. Von Blerke, and Mike Papini, and Mary Scott now Summers, and David, and Wyndham Farrar, and Sophy Brent. And not for the first time I watched and wondered at the seemingly simultaneous and independent workings of so many bits of machinery that seemed to be me, and that seemed to make up, on a larger scale (all life being an emblem of all other life), society. And I wondered whether I was right to pay such attention to the part of me that responded with disturbing eagerness to the overtures of a man like Wyndham Farrar, for what was it that responded in this way but the physical rubbish of me, the blood and skin and so forth, and a whole heap of tatty romantic notions picked up from our tatty sexual decadence? Because reason as I might, and as I did, it was this part, this dark and wanting part, that seemed to have reality, that seemed to tug and suck and pull at the rest of me with overriding need.

At the end of the show the applause was enthusiastic, as was to be expected. The play itself was highly entertaining, and not a laugh had been missed. There were cheers and bravos, and when the noise began to die away the moment happened that I had been waiting for: the moment of the speech. It was delivered by some civic dignitary, who thanked the cast for a delightful evening, and Selwyn for his direction, and the architect for his design and above all for the easy access to bars at intervals (laughter), and Wyndham Farrar, who had greatly distinguished the undertaking by his co-operation and enthusiasm, and whose own productions were eagerly awaited; and then he thanked those who had made the venture possible, the Arts Council of Great Britain, various local donors, "but above all Mrs. Charlotte Von Blerke, to whose generosity this building and this whole enterprise owe their existence, and without whose help we should not be here tonight.

"Unfortunately, Mrs. Von Blerke herself has been prevented by illness from being with us tonight, which I am sure will grieve us as much as it will doubtless grieve her, for I know how much she has cherished the idea of this theatre and how closely she has followed all our plans and discussions. We can only hope that she will be able to be with us at the opening of the next production, in a few days' time. In the meantime we can only deplore her absence, wish her a speedy return to health and thank her for the inestimable value of the gift which she has bestowed upon our city."

And the audience applauded dutifully the dead wet lady, who floated from some fishlike watery depths of coincidence across the trivial, sentimental drama of my life.

There was a party after the show, on stage, with champagne and all, which Mike and Dave and I duly attended. It was not very amusing, and was distinguished for me by the extraordi-

narily brave and gay behaviour of Sophy, who
wandered around in a gold-and-brown dress,
still covered in the reckless patches that she
had worn on stage, pretending that she was a
great success, which not only was the best way
out for her, but also let everyone else off very
easily. Wyndham still had his middle-aged
couple in tow; he introduced them to Dave and
me at one point, and it appeared that the smart
woman was his sister, and her husband something to do with some huge chemical industry.
My eyes kept meeting Wyndham's with embarrassing frequency, even when we were at a
considerable distance from each other. The
other thing that happened was that Mike Papini made a pass at me: he got me in a quiet
corner in the wings, while Dave and Sophy were
being photographed together by the press, and
told me that I shouldn't spend my time with a
shallow egocentric like Dave, that I had no
right to live in a backwater like Hereford and
why didn't I come back to London and live
with him. He must have been quite sincere
because he started to stammer, a thing I had
not heard him do since his first novel came
out. I was astounded, and said that I had no
intention of doing anything of the sort, and
that anyway, didn't he realize I had two children. He replied that surely children were quite
easily dealt with, he thought we had a nanny,
and they could stay in the country, couldn't
they, it was good for them, and we could go
and catch a late night train immediately, if
there was one. I said he must have gone crazy,
there was no train, we hadn't got a nanny, we
had an inefficient French girl, and that in any

case, I couldn't bear to be separated from my children for more than a day at a time. He thought that that was pretty feeble, and said so; whereat I said:

"Look here, Mike, the truth is that you couldn't tell the difference between a child and a kitten," and walked briskly away.

I walked briskly all the way home. I was by no means displeased by Mike's overtures, though I was surprised. It would take someone very negligible to displease me. It seemed quite amazing that I should have had two overtures of more or less the same nature within one week, when for three years nobody except men on building sites had paid tribute to my inaccessible charms. I suppose that my encounter with Wyndham had loosed around me a sense of restlessness or availability, which, together with the champagne, had put the idea of me into Mike Papini's head. And now I had a choice. Not that there was any question of what I would choose, for Mike had so many qualities that I seriously valued and Wyndham so many that seriously disquieted me that I knew that with an obstinate desire like mine for violation I could choose nothing but Wyndham. I amused myself as I walked through the dripping rain of May by totting up their differences, and what it all came down to was that Mike Papini was a professional and Wyndham Farrar an amateur. Mike Papini, whatever the vast differences of background and attitude, came from the same home as Mary Scott: to him life was a discipline, a search for values, an investigation of the soul, an apprenticeship to a trade, and all his aberrations were simply an effort to conduct his affairs according to some notion, however strange, of the right way. Whereas with Wyndham I felt that life was an entertainment.

The next morning, at about eleven, I was surprised to receive a visit from Sophy Brent. It was an hour when I had always imagined her to be in bed. I was doing the washing when she arrived. Pascal let her in, and as she sat down on the kitchen table, looking unusually pale and gloomy, I wondered what could have upset her.

"You're up early," I said brightly, as she did not seem to want to say anything herself. I was too busy fishing boiling-hot nappies out of the washing machine with a pair of wooden tongs to approach her with more finesse. She did not reply, so I said nothing more. I could hardly have heard her if she had spoken, as the hot tap was running and the noise of the gas is deafening. When I turned the tap off, she said in a subdued voice:

"David got a smashing notice in the *Telegraph*," and I suddenly realized what her arrival implied: she had come to be consoled for her bad reviews. I had paid very little attention to the morning papers; indeed, I had seen only two of them, but in both there had been inauspicious mentions of Sophy's lack of experience and inadequate technique, and as these two papers were the civilized ones, I could well guess what those daily headline drama critics who pride themselves on the annihilating phrase might have found to say.

"Oh, really?" I said. "I haven't seen any of the papers yet," and I started to punch the nap-

pies up and down to emphasize that I had no
time for the press. I had already told her at
the party how wonderful and marvellous I had
thought she was, and I did not want to go
through all that again. Her depression upset
me: it is so unmistakable, the misery of wanting nothing but success and not getting it. I
wondered what mechanism of defence she had
set in action, but she hardly seemed to have
got into her stride. She talked for a little about
what people had said the night before and the
dress Natalie had been wearing, and as she
talked I remembered all the shades of disappointment I had been forced to witness before,
ranging from the pathetic, through the crude
and brusque, to the violent. Eventually she
came out with it.

"You'd hardly believe it," she said, "but do
you know what the *Clarion* said about Felicity?
It said her performance was a masterpiece of
comic invention. Have you ever heard anything
so ridiculous? Honestly, Felicity—I think she's
the world's worst, don't you?"

"I didn't think she was very good," I said
warily, paying close attention to my task.

"No, honestly, Emma, she really is bloody
awful, if you ask me. All that arm-waving, and
did you see that fantastic make-up she was
wearing? That puce lipstick she wears makes her
face look bright blue on stage, it really does."

"Well, it is a character part, after all," I said.

"Yes, I know it is, but there's no need to
look more hideous than you can help, is there?
David thinks she's awful, he told me so himself."

"He thinks most people are awful."

"Do you think so? I think he's the only nice person in the company. He's the only person who ever has a good word to say for anyone, if you ask me. Everyone else is just mean and boring. You are lucky, having a husband like him."

"Yes," I said.

"Is he in at the moment? Could I see him, do you think?"

"He's in bed, actually, but if you just hang on a minute till I've finished this lot I'll make us all a cup of coffee and we can go and get him up."

I glanced expressively at the gas stove as I spoke, heaved a sigh and made a great show of turning the mangle. But I knew it would be no use, the thought of putting the kettle on did not even flit near the outskirts of her mind. With complete absorption she sat there, and after a pause went on:

"Everyone told me it would be such an opportunity, working here with Wyndham Farrar and all that, but I just think it's jolly boring, that't what I think. Why does everyone think Wyndham's so bloody marvellous?"

"Do they think that?"

"Well, they seem to, don't they? I quite liked him at first, he used to be all over me, darling this and darling that, but now he hardly seems to notice I'm around."

"It'll be different," I said, "in his next production. You've got quite a decent part in that, haven't you? He probably just hasn't had time for you so far."

"Do you think that's what it is? I suppose he has been a bit busy. I don't suppose you've really had time to meet him yet, have you? David seems to think quite a lot of him. But he does make some frightful mistakes. What about casting Viola as Zanche, don't you think that's fantastic?"

"I haven't seen *The White Devil* yet," I said, "so I really couldn't say." I hate the sight of such ordinary pain and meanness. "And if you don't mind moving over," I went on, "I'll get the coffee out of the cupboard now."

And I made the coffee, and as David refused to get out of bed I sent her in to him. I did not grudge him his task of trying to persuade her she was a good actress, in the face of such a general agreement of opinion and against what I felt sure must be his own judgement. As I watched the soapy water from the machine drain away into the sink, I reflected that I, who had felt cheered by the tentative and probably halfhearted advances of a neurotic novelist, was contemplating keeping some sort of hold over a man like Wyndham Farrar, who had infinite choice and infinite opportunity, whereas I could not even think up a plausible excuse for a five-minute telephone call. I felt real envy of Sophy Brent, with her small lonely flatlet and her gas ring, her heaps of odd stockings, her drawers full of old gritty lipsticks, her empty evenings, her unwatched tears in bed. I felt that if for Wyndham there was any question of choice between her and me, she would win.

What was wrong with me, I wondered, what had happened to me, that I, who had seemed cut out for some extremity or other, should be here now bending over a washing machine to

pick out a button or two and some bits of soggy
wet cotton? What chances were there now for
the once-famous Emma, whose name had been
in certain small exclusive circles the cause for
so much discussion and prediction? They would
not think much of me now, I thought, if they
could see me, those Marxists in Rome, those
historians and photographers in Hampstead,
those undergraduates in two universities.
There were more odds against me than there
had been against Mrs. Von Blerke, and she
had gone under.

10

THE first night of *The White Devil* was a close
social repetition of the first night of *The Clandestine Marriage*: I wore the same dress, a
dingy cement-coloured thing, Mike Papini
arrived on the same train, complained in the
same words about the journey and we went
and sat in the same seats. The only differences
lay in the play itself and in the fact that the
death of Mrs. Von Blerke had by now been
announced. Presumably, this play being a
bloody tragedy, they thought its acknowledge-
ment would augment and not detract from
the atmosphere. And this time Wyndham did
not sit in front of me, though his sister and

her husband did. He was presumably busy elsewhere.

The play impressed me, despite myself: such fury, such destruction, such passion, and everyone acting well because, as Wyndham had said, they all thought they had the best parts; and as Wyndham had also said, David really had got the best part. As I watched him I saw at last why we were here in Hereford, why David had brought me here: to play this role in this obscure play he had been willing to submit me to unlimited boredom and fresh air and, as he might have foreseen, to infidelity. He justified himself, too. I felt, while watching, that it was worth it. In the last scene of the play, in his last, dying speech, he had some lines that came closer to him than anything I had ever heard him say on stage before: "I do not look," he said clutching at his mock wound,

"Who went before nor who shall follow me. No, at myself I will begin and end."

And the way he delivered this, and the whole accompanying scene, was quite tremendous. He had in them the exultant satisfaction which was the reason for his being an actor. All he wanted from life was to be able to express, like this, in public, to a mass of quiet people, what he felt himself to be. It was not merely pleasure that he had there on stage: it was a sense of clarity, a feeling of being, by words and situations not of his own making, defined and confined, so that his power and his energy could meet together in one great explanatory moment. It was not enough for David that I should try to understand him or that his friends and employers should understand him, for we subjected him by the pressure of our needs and opinions to amorphous confusion: what he wanted was nothing less than total public clarity.

And this time he had achieved it. Everyone agreed that his performance had been remarkable, and the whole production was received with rapture. At the party afterwards, which was held in Wyndham's own flat, people called Wyndham a genius and Dave the greatest actor since I don't know who, and Dave got horribly drunk, and so did I. It was a much less decorous party than the one after *The Clandestine Marriage*, as there were far fewer local people there and everyone drank too much. I hardly spoke to Wyndham, except to tell him that I had been impressed by his production, to which he said:

"How grudging you are, Emma. Of course it was good, of course you were impressed. Who do you think I am that I shouldn't have got it right? I only did this piece because I'm the only man in England capable of putting it on."

Everyone seemed to be in the same mood of tipsy self-aggrandizement, except for Michael Fenwick, who had grown tearful. At about two in the morning David began to quarrel with everyone, and when he started to pitch into Julian, saying things like "You can't sit on the fence forever, why don't you take a good look in the mirror and decide to kick that schoolboy conscience of yours down the stairs for good and all and enjoy yourself?" I decided to get out.

I walked home, alone, once more alone. I am always walking home alone, and this is one of the things I foresaw and thought I would enjoy when I first married.. A kind of rage was inside me. When I reached the bridge, there was a swan drifting downstream on the wide river, and the tranquillity of the image, compared with the smoky heat that I had left, filled me with hopelessness.

When I got back, I had to crawl up the stairs on hands and knees, I was so tired from drink and prolonged insufficiency of sleep. When I reached my bedroom, I stared into the mirror of that hideous dressing table at my own chilly face and I said aloud "Wyndham" to see what the word would sound like, let loose from the furtive hutch of my mind. It sounded bloody silly, and my face and lips intoning it looked ridiculous. I started to tear off my clothes, furiously, muttering to myself, "Bloody stupid ridiculous names they have, Wyndham, Wyndham, David Evans, what a pair of conceited pathetic self-deluding fools, what *folie de grandeur*. They don't seem to realize that the theatre is a dead end, a minority art, that nobody ever goes to it but actors and actors' wives; they think they've done something clever now, those two, they think they're famous just because they've got a few columns in the daily press. *How grudging you are, Emma, how grudging you are, don't you know I'm a great man?* Oh yes, oh yes, a pretty pointless kind of greatness, too, being a director, and why should I be taken in by it? I know it's not real, I know that that kind of fame is just the top tenth of the iceberg and that the rest of life, real fame, real power, is nothing like this at all, I know they don't count, pop arts and film stars and knights and dames and duchesses and Percy Edward Fararr, F.R.C.S., and Laura Montefiore, I know all that, and why should I even listen? But I do listen, I do listen, I am the perfect audience, I do more than listen, I depend. For love, and bread and butter, and company, I depend. On the cheap, the *louche*, the tawdry, the shiny, the glistening caratless shammy selling line."

In the morning Dave and I lay in bed covered by a crackling sea of newsprint: we had every daily paper there with us, and Flora as well, who was crawling around on it and ripping at random. In every paper David had a good notice: nobody had missed him out. He lay back on the pillows swamped with goodwill, swamped with his own importance, and encouraged Flora to tear up the reviews, handsome photographs and all. He affected not to read or notice critics, and was pleased to see her disposing with such vigour of these signs of his glory and his shame. She was overjoyed by his good spirits, and leaped on him and pulled the hair on his chest and stuffed paper in his ears; and as I lay and watched them, half dazed with sleep, I felt from a long way off an immense forgiveness of him and hope for forgiveness from him; nothing near, nothing present, but the awareness of some distant factual understanding, as though I knew him

too well not at some point to sympathize with
what he was feeling.

Once the excitement of the first nights was
over and my varying moods of admiration and
disgust had passed, I found myself reduced to
an absurd state, of which the cause was un-
doubtedly Wyndham Farrar. I began to count
the hours until I might see him again, as I had
counted hours at school. Events flowed around
me in a strange meaningless surge: we ate, we
slept, we talked, I went shopping, I fed my
children and I felt perpetually drunk. I used to
be like that when I was sixteen, when nothing,
nothing could touch me; when the paltry nature of my life at school and home, compared
with my vast expectations, reduced me to a
state of sleepwalking paralysis. And now, too,
David seemed as unreal and as encumbering a
shadow as my sick mother had once seemed;
and as for my babies, I could hardly believe
that I had ever had them. They smiled at me
and I smiled at them as I smile at babies in
the park, strange babies; and this was real
pain.

I do not know how I managed to get through
the days until my next meeting with Wyndham. Time seemed to have gone wrong: it had
not exactly stopped still, but it had turned
thick, like mud or treacle, so that getting
through it required great exertion. When the
day and the hour finally arrived, I had to admit that, despite my self-pity and my domestic
worries, my opportunities for liaison were far
greater than those of most women. It was very
simple. David left the house for the theatre
at half past six; I had time to bathe Flora and

to give Joe his bottle and to get changed before going out to meet Wyndham on a street corner, having told Pascal that I was going to the cinema. It could hardly have been easier: but for the rubbish that I carried along with me in my mind I was as free as anyone is to go anywhere.

The evening began rather disastrously. After so much expectation I was overcome with doubt when I actually set eyes on the man. He seemed to think we had left things at a more advanced stage than I had thought, and before we were ten miles out of town a certain amount of hand-slapping, wincing and muttering had already taken place. When we drew up for dinner, I was feeling both nervous and mean. I wondered what I had let myself in for, and I began to think, now that I had clearly for the next few hours at least got him, that I did not even like him. I have still come to very little conclusion on that point, so thoroughly does passion obscure one's sense of identity. For there can be no mistake, passion certainly seemed to be somewhere around, and although it may seem ludicrous to talk in such circumstances of Venus attached to her prey, such were the literary allusions which arose from time to time in my mind. For I hung on his every word and gesture: every compliment enchanted me, every glance unclothed me, and yet I could not deceive myself that it was him, himself, that I liked. For one thing, he was a frightful namedropper: most of his anecdotes had some real perceptive or narrative interest, but he ruined at least half of them by nonchalantly including the name of some unmistakably world-famous figure. Of course he knew these people: I did not doubt that he knew these people, but what was the necessity for telling me so? It diminished him, his insistence on his own importance. I sat there in mingled delight and irritation, fiddling with my *sole Véronique* and wishing from time to time that he would just shut up.

When we left after the meal, it was not yet dark. He did not want to linger over coffee, and I thought with apprehension that I knew why not, but when we got into the car all he said was:

"We could go for a drive now; there's a place near here I'd like to show you. You don't have to be back yet, do you?"

"I ought to be back by half past eleven," I said, but it was only just after nine. The thought of going for a drive appealed to me: it postponed things, and it was a lovely evening, with a lot of clouds blowing across the sky in a hurry. But we did not drive very far. After a few miles along roads that seemed too narrow for the car Wyndham drew up in a place that seemed to be nowhere, but which turned out to be a very small village. I could see from the car a church on a sharply rising slope, and we had stopped by a high brick wall.

"Where on earth is this?" I said as I looked round. I felt that he had some trick up his sleeve, as indeed he had.

"This is a village," he said. "The house behind this wall belongs to my aunt. I thought we might go and have a look at it."

"Will she be there?" I said, unable to think of anything else to say.

"No, she won't," said Wyndham. "She's dead.

I think the house is for sale. I wanted to have a look at it before they ruin it. Would you like to come and see?"

"Of course I would," I said, wondering by what chance or stroke of intuition he had struck on so precisely the kind of excursion that has for me an irresistible charm.

Even the wall itself looked promising: the brick was a pale overgrown red, and it glowed with varying inner shades in the fading light. We got out, and I followed him to the gates. I was wearing high-heeled shoes, and they sank into the grass and mud at every step. At the end of the wall, just before the gate, there was a For Sale notice: *The Residence known as Binneford House,* it said, *situated at Binneford, formerly the property of Miss Marjorie Farrar, will be put up for auction on June 16, together with the gardener's cottage and twelve acres of land.* I stopped to read the description of the central heating and the reception rooms while Wyndham went on alone. When I finally followed him and rounded the corner of the drive, I saw him standing there, and behind him this extraordinary house. It was huge, and so beautiful that I was stunned: a large, early eighteenth-century house of a massive, delicate elegance, the stone pink and grey, the paint-work white on the doors and the innumerable leaded and perfectly proportioned windows and the whole thing overgrown with the most ordered profusion of climbing plants. We must have been two hundred yards away at that first view, and we could take it in as it had been built, as it had been designed, controlled by the architect's intention.

I took Wyndham's arm, and we started to walk slowly up the pebbled drive towards it. There was a lawn on one side of us, and on the other a shrubbery full of trees and flowers, daffodils and narcissis, all faintly gleaming and exhaling in the quickly gathering darkness. When we reached the front door, Wyndham said:

"I haven't got a key, there's nobody here, I hope you don't mind if we don't go in."

"I don't mind," I said.

I wanted him to tell me about it, but I was afraid to ask him, for he seemed moody and removed, as though he were thinking, and not about me. We wandered round to the back of the house, peering through the windows at the dust sheets and the marble fireplaces: the garden stretched away downhill on the far side, through a jumble of scrub and bushes, and Wyndham waved a hand in that direction and said:

"That's the river, down there."

"What river?" I said.

"What river do you think? The Wye. The River Wye. Do you want to go and have a look? It's probably very muddy down there, and as far as I can remember, it's all covered with nettles. You'd ruin your stockings."

"I don't mind about my stockings."

"Don't you? Let's go and see then." So I scrambled down the steep bank after him. The garden just fell away in a tangle of nothingness towards the river's edge. When we got to the bottom, we stood there in the thick wet grass staring at the swirling water. The river was very full from the continual rain of spring, and it

was rushing over the roots of the trees in a
solid, eddying mass. As we stood there and
watched it, I began to feel cold, and then to
feel frightened: it was quite dark by now, although our eyes had grown accustomed to the
darkness, and the silent insect-filled damp of
the evening was quite foreign to me, quite
beyond my control. There was nothing within
reach that I understood. Here I was, in the
midst of all the greenery that I had mocked
at with my friends in London, and I was un-
nerved by it. It seemed more real than London,
the river and the trees and the grass, so much
profusion, so much of everything, and not a
human being in reach, not a person to watch it.
I shivered so that Wyndham would notice, and
he said:

"It is cold, isn't it? Come on, let's go." He
pulled me after him back up the bank and
into the cultivated part of the garden.

On the way I stumbled on something soft and
brown and frightful, which felt like a dead
mouse, but when I bent down to see what it
was I found it was only an apple, a wet and
rotten apple that had lain there since the
autumn before. It occurred to me that this was
the course of nature, for apples to fall off trees
and lie and rot in the grass, and that the
other thing, the thing with which I was familiar, the picking and the eating and the selling was a much later development. When we
got back into the car, Wyndham said:

"Well, I suppose that'll be the last time I'll
go there. I used to come here when I was a
boy, to stay with her."

"I'm cold," I said. "Give me a cigarette."

"Didn't you like it, Emma?"

"Of course I liked it. It's just so odd, to think of all this lying around out here and not a soul to look at it, and in London every blade of grass has to struggle to survive. Every tree has to win a battle against the County Council."

"Don't you like this better?"

"Not really. I think I like London better. I feel out of place here."

"I used to like it here when I was a child."

"It must be different now."

"No. It hasn't changed much. There was a phase when it seemed smaller: when I was seventeen or so I used to come back here and think that it had shrunk. But then it grew again. After the war it grew again.

"It was your expectations that had shrunk."

"How well you put it. Yes, that was exactly what had happened. When I was seventeen I wanted everything. But after the war I was glad to see a house standing."

"It makes me feel a child to hear you talk of the war."

"You are a child."

"No. Not quite. I have children of my own."

"Emma."

"Yes?"

"Talking of shrinking, I think you must have been deceiving me."

"Whatever do you mean?"

"Well, I trust you won't mind my mentioning it, but when I first saw you I remember thinking. Here is an extraordinary girl, she's as thin as a stick everywhere else, but she has the most terrific breasts. And now they don't seem

terrific any more. In the size sense, I mean. Size-
wise."

I started to laugh.

"Do you mean you only asked me out because I was a freak?"

"Not at all. You're a freak anyway, breasts
or no breasts. But tell me what happened to
them, why did I get the impression that they
were so splendid?"

"Oh, it's very simple, really, the explanation. I stopped feeding Joseph, that's all.
Breast-feeding, ever heard of it? They go
down again when you stop, quite suddenly.
Didn't you know?"

"I suppose I must have known. I never
thought of it, that's all. I've never seen anyone
feed a baby. Except my sister, and she gave it
up after a week; she didn't like it, or something.
Do you mean to say they just collapse, straight-
away?"

"More or less. They don't collapse, really, you
know, they just go back to where they were
before. Don't you like them now?"

"Of course I like them. I like you altogether.
It's just that what I said to myself was, Here's
a girl with no blood in her veins and big breasts
and as thin as a stick and taller than I am. Pro-
vocative, don't you think?"

"That's what Dave used to say, that I had no
blood in my veins. One day he got his razor
blade and cut my wrist, just to see."

"What happened?"

"It bled. That was before we were married."

"Of course."

"Of course."

"Emma."

"Yes?" "Undo your coat. Undo your dress. I won't touch you, I just want to look at you."

I unbuttoned the front of my coat and the front of my shirt, and sat there in my black lace brassiere, with the moonlight falling on my dun skin, a smooth lunar landscape. He stared at me, and I stared at myself for a while, and then up at the wild romantic sky, where the clouds were still hurrying with the same fluid violence as the brown river. After a while Wyndham said:

"Emma, I like them small. I really do," and I said:

"I'm glad, because I do, too. Though they look a bit tired, don't you think?"

"You always look tired, all of you. Doesn't he let you get enough sleep?"

"It's the babies. They don't let me sleep."

"Poor Emma. That doesn't seem right, somehow."

"Wyndham, I'd better be going or I'll be late. Now that you mention them."

And so we set off. On the way back he suddenly said, "I wonder what I would have thought if I had known then that one day I'd be sitting outside with a girl like you," and I felt that I had once more become a background, though that was fair enough, for he had become a background for me, too. I thought I would not reply, but after about five minutes' silence I said:

"Had you any idea then of where you would be by now?" and he said:

"Oh, I used to be ambitious. In those days."

We did not get back, despite my constant reminders, until after the usual time for

David's return. Wyndham dropped me at the end of the street, promising to phone, and I ran home thinking of excuses. However, there was no occasion for excuses, for the moment that I flung open the door I smelled a strong and unmistakable odour of gas. Indeed, it was so strong that it seemed to greet me through the keyhole. I flew up the stairs and into the kitchen. The air was thick with it, and I could tell from the noise before I got there that the oven was on, unlit. I switched it off, pulled open the window and retreated; the whole house stank. The sitting room light was on, so I went in and found David sitting on the sofa reading some theatrical magazine. He looked up blankly as I entered, and said at the sight of my face:

"Hello, Emma, what's the matter?"

"What the hell do you think you're doing?" I yelled. "Are you trying to commit suicide or something? The whole place is full of gas. Can't you smell it?"

"Gas?" he said dozily, and with extreme placidity. "Is it really? Oh, is that what it is? I thought there was a funny smell when I came in. I have got a bit of a headache, come to think of it. Do you think that's what it is?"

"You must be out of your mind," I said. "You must be crazy. How long have you been sitting in all this?"

"I've only been in for about ten minutes."

"You're lucky you're not dead," I said, and strode along the corridor to Pascal's room, and for the first time in our acquaintance beat rudely on her door. I felt pushed into noise and action by the awful sleepy languor of the house. A feeble voice answered me, and I opened the door. She was not dead, but she was lying in bed looking like wax, with sweat in beads on her yellow face.

"What on earth's the matter?" I said, and she moaned:

"*Mon dieu, je fais mal. J'ai mal de tête.*"

"I should bloody well think so," I said, forgetting in the heat of the moment about kindness to foreigners and watching in horror the broad pale mess of her usually pert features. "The house is absolutely full of gas. Whatever have you been doing?"

"I have done nothing," she said weakly. "Nothing at all."

"Oh, then who was it?" I said as I tried to wrench her windows open. She looked appalled by the idea: to her fresh air was deadlier than gas. "You might have been dead," I went on angrily. "I can't think what you can have been doing. The oven was on at number nine. Oh Christ, I suppose it must have been Flora. Was she playing in the kitchen while I was giving Joseph his bottle?"

"Yes, yes, she was, she must have done it," said Pascal, and incomprehensibly started to giggle. "What a naughty girl," she said. "Naughty little Flora, trying to kill us all."

"Do you mean," I said, "that you didn't even notice? That since seven o'clock you haven't noticed a thing?"

"I did not notice anything, no. I sit in the sitting room, and about eight o'clock I start a headache, so I go into the kitchen and have a whisky, then I feel worse, so I have another or two, and then I go to bed."

"Oh Jesus, Jesus, Jesus," I said, too angry to

laugh, although she seemed quite ready to see the funny side of it, if only I would give her a lead. "You must be an idiot," I said. "What if I'd stayed out all night? You'd probably all have been dead by the morning. I bet you feel bloody awful, with all that whisky on top of all that gas. I'd better go and look at the children."

"Oh, they will be OK," she said, lying back on her pillow with a pale and guiltless smile.

Outside Flora's door I hesitated, wondering whether it was worth taking the risk of waking her just to see whether she had been gassed or not. When I crept in she seemed to be peacefully asleep and breathing normally, so I opened the window and left her. I went to bed feeling, as one might imagine, indispensable, and remembering the kind of phrase that Mrs. Scott used to utter in moments of irritation, such as "You'd forget to breathe if I didn't remind you" and "If I didn't put the food in front of you, you'd all starve to death," remarks that now seemed to me to have some point. Had it not happened to me, I could not have believed that two tolerably responsible adults could behave with such lunacy, and I knew that I myself was temperamentally incapable of such a lapse. If there was a gas tap on, I would be the one to switch it off. I tried to explain to David before we fell asleep that but for me his children might have been dead, and curiously enough, he did not think of asking me where I had been for the rest of the evening.

11

THE next week summer arrived. The weather
suddenly changed: the rain stopped, the sun
came out and Wyndham did not ring. For days
and days I did not hear of or from him, so that
I retraced every word of our last encounter
and regretted every nuance of irritation on my
part: I wished I had listened to his account of
Sir Somebody's second marriage with more eagerness. Then I heard by accident that he was
in London. I thought that he might at least
have let me know. I was left with summer on
my hands and nothing to do with it. I noticed
that the air had grown warm, that coats had
been discarded for sunglasses, that the cathedral now looked gay, not gloomy, and that the
earth swarmed with vegetation; and I also noticed that these things no longer gave me the
childish, total satisfaction that they had given
me for the last few years. I seemed to be back
once more in some kind of adolescence, in that
stage when I could not tell one season from
another and was estranged from any external
event like sunshine: I was shut up once more
in an artificial world of waiting. It did not help
me that I could hardly believe it: it seemed so
improbable that a sensible, active person like

myself should be listening night and day for
the telephone, jumping at the sight of the
name Farrar on a noticeboard and walking
along every street as though there were someone behind me. Incredulity and expectation
strung me up between them, and I could let go
of neither.

It is boring, perhaps, if I repeat that I had
no way of passing the time. Only those with
small children can appreciate how little and
how much they occupy the mind and the day.
David was not at this point rehearsing, but he
was playing every evening and two matinees a
week, and spent most of the rest of the time in
the pub. One day I went out for a walk. David
had taken Flora to the barber's with him, Joe
was asleep in his pram and Pascal was washing
her hair, so that I thought that now it was
summer it was my duty to go for a walk. I
started off with the cathedral, where I inspected the Mappa Mundi, the tomb of Chan-
cellor Swinefield with its sixteen gaily dressed
small pigs; I was followed on this visit by two
fair-haired pale, squiffy youths, wearing shiny
black boots and pale blue jeans with the bot-
toms rolled up, who went round the place
trying every locked door and window. They
were giggling to themselves, and I could not
decide whether I was their audience or whether I was simply negligible. I watched them
with unobtrusive dignity. I could predict, after
a few assays, their every movement, just as with
Flora I could see in advance which hassock she
would next unhook, which steps she would as-
cend, into which hole she would thrust her finger. Their crowning effort arrived when we

reached the font, a huge solid ancient piece of stone, covered with a mighty lid. I walked past it, then stopped to read an inscription on the wall. They followed me, until the font attracted their delinquent attention; the larger of the boys, with one eye on me and the other on his task, advanced on it and took hold of the great iron ring on top of the lid. The younger said something like "Go on, you never," whereat, like a film Hercules, the boy heaved at it and got it up. He held it triumphantly in the air, six inches above the stone basin, with a tremendous look of satisfaction, before he let it thud back into position. I was very impressed. I openly watched. When I moved off again, towards the door, they started to follow me once more. I was just about to go out when, amidst much giggling and whispering, one of them said, more to the other than to me:

"You from the theatre, miss?"

"In a way," I said, not turning round, but not wishing to be misleading.

"Thought you was, miss," said the other. "Mind if we walk along with you a bit, miss?"

"I don't suppose so," I said as we emerged from the leathery interior into the sunlight, "though I don't suppose we'd get very far, would we? I'm going to the shops now, anyway."

"Oh, OK.," they said, and slouched off in the other direction, their hands resting neatly in their trouser pockets upon their bony hips. I said good-bye, but they did not respond. I liked the insolence of their deference. And I reflected, as I wandered aimlessly towards the town, that these words were the first social words that I had exchanged with any of the inhabitants of Hereford. I had bought things, it is true, and changed my library book, but I had said nothing. I had met nobody, I was living in a small dissociated pocket of people who had settled in this town and who had no more connection with it than they had with any other town in England. When autumn came they would move on, and that would be that. And the town itself, which seemed to outsiders to be a unit, was made up of pockets of people, all as unrelated to one another as actors to farmers or as farmers to "teds" in blue jeans. All that connected people was buying and selling. There was the cathedral, with its vergers and deans and choir-boys; and the theatre, with its actors and directors and stagehands; and the market, with its farmers and butchers and beef; and the library, with its librarians; and the newspaper, with its owners and its journalists and its printers; all little disconnected cells, and within each cell there are laws and habits and a prescribed language, and prescribed jokes. I wondered for a moment, as I walked along, whether I did not perhaps hate the place so much because of its so fully occupied and classified air. Unlike London, it left no room for the placeless, and I felt a moment's piercing nostalgia for my school, which was the only place in my life where I had been fully classified, fully accounted for and fully known. Since then I had learned so well to detach myself from any attempt at a group: I had learned so thoroughly the tone of voice that dissociates, the glance that discourages, the slight formidable mystification which leaves one unaccounted for in the vast arrangements of human kind. I had refused to live in a street with anyone who could contaminate me by similarity, I had refused to wear the clothes that might have accounted for me or to pursue the interests that might have created me. And I had ended a freak, with nothing to my credit but my difference. I thought bitterly about that job that I might have been doing which would have been so thoroughly public and so anonymous; and my fury with David, who had brought me up so abruptly against my own weakness and against the cozy settling instincts of others, increased and smouldered.

I had arrived by now in a small and ancient back street, not far from where we lived, where I had previously discovered an interesting junk shop. I had not been in the time before, but now I had some money on me and I thought I would go and buy something. It was a long time since I had bought anything. So I went in and started to look around: there were many flowery cheese dishes, of which I already possessed four, and I was wondering whether to add to my collection when I caught sight of a small pillar, which was supporting one end of a bench covered with old overpriced Woolworth's glass dishes. It was a very nice slender small pillar, about three feet high, in an interesting gray marble and with a miniature Corinthian top. It seemed to have been somewhat abridged, but the proportions of it, as it stood, were very appealing. I did not think that anything so entirely useless could be very valuable, and I called for the proprietor, who was

drinking tea in his back sitting room. I asked
him if the pillar was for sale. Oh yes, he said,
I could have it for fifteen pounds. Good heavens, I said, it didn't look as though it was
worth anything like that to me, whereat he
said it was a very nice small pillar, very decorative, and what did I want it for? As I only
wanted it because it was a nice small pillar
and very decorative, I could not think of an
answer, but I got him to move the bench off
the top of it so that I could have a good look.
He hung around all the time, saying things like
"It's a very good bit of marble, that" and
"Could make a nice sundial, that could,"
though the truth is that he could never before
have tried to sell such an unsaleable object. The
top was very rough, and covered with old plaster. I knew that I was going to buy it, I knew
that I was even going to pay fifteen pounds
for it if he made me, as I had already worked
out that it would look very good underneath
my marble bust of Lady Mary Wortley-Mon-
tagu. I felt crazy, and horribly in touch with
my own craziness.

The poor man could not work out for what
reason I could possibly want it, so he could not
decide on a selling line. He kept mentioning
gardens until I said that I had no garden, and
then he was silenced. I asked him where it had
come from. He was very cagey, and said he
thought it had come from one of the big houses
roundabouts and that he had had it for a long
time.

"I don't really want to part with it," he said
hastily, after this admission. "That's why I've
had it so long; it comes in kind of handy,

propping up that table, you know. I'll be in a bit of a difficulty with that table if you decide to take it."

Finally I bought it for twelve pounds, and consoled myself that it would have cost twice as much in Camden Passage. I wanted to get it home immediately, I was full of such spurious excitement, and he was so stunned by my folly that he said he would take it round for me himself in his van. I watched him loading it: he had just managed to heave it on and was about to set off when light suddenly appeared to dawn. He leaned out of his window with the joy of deduction in every feature and said:

"I know where you're from, you're from that new theatre, aren't you? You'll be the what-do-you-call it, the property mistress, won't you? Look, if there's any more of this old-fashioned stuff I can be helping you with, just you let me know. I'll get you a card," and he got out of his cab and rushed back into his back sitting room, and reappeared some time later with an old yellow engraved card. "That's my firm," he said. "Look, that's the name of my firm. E. G. Spode. He was my father. I haven't had any new cards done for a long time, I never seemed to get around to it, but the address is the same, the name's the same, that's the main thing, isn't it?"

"Oh yes," I said, "I should have thought that was what mattered most."

"Well, exactly," he said, very pleased. "That's just what I say. Anyway, miss, if there's anything else you want, just you let me know and I'll most likely be able to get it for you."

"I'll let you know," I said, and he set off. I walked very slowly homewards. The longer I stayed out, the more chance there was that Wyndham might have come back from London and rung me in my absence. I wondered if Pascal would be very surprised by the delivery of a small marble pillar. When I did get back, it was not Pascal who was round, but David, in a very bad temper and with hair aggressively short.

"What on earth have they done to your hair?" I said mildly, to forestall whatever was coming. He did not reply, naturally, but threw all the vigour of his annoyance with the barber into his opening accusation.

"What on earth do you mean," he said, "by having marble pillars delivered round here whenever I'm out? What in God's name do you want that thing for? Haven't we got enough junk in the house already? There's hardly room to move as it is, you can't put an ashtray down without moving something first."

"Don't you like it?" I said, gazing at it with some pride; it was standing on a piece of newspaper in the middle of the drawing room floor.

"Like it? What on earth is there to like about a lump like that? It's just a chunk of old stone."

"It's not stone, it's marble."

"Well, marble then. I don't like marble, it looks like liver sausage."

"That's red marble, not grey marble. You might at least bother to look at it before you complain about it."

"I've been looking at it for the last five minutes. I've never seen anything so ridiculous in my life."

"They've cut your hair terribly short this time, haven't they, David?"

"Yes, they have, and I'll tell you why. It was because that wretched daughter of yours was larking round so much that I couldn't keep an eye on what he was doing to me. I'm never going to take her out again."

"You suggested taking her this time, not me. She's always very good with me."

"Oh yes, very bloody likely. And how much did you give for that load of rubbish?"

"Twelve pounds, and five bob delivery money."

"What did you say?"

"Twelve pounds, and five bob delivery money."

"You must be out of your mind."

"Do you think so?"

"And whose money did you pay for that with? The house-keeping? Do you really think I'm going to slave away night and day so that you can go out and buy useless, hideous objects at prices that suggest that you ought to have your head seen to?"

"I'll pay you back."

"Oh, will you. What out of?"

"My next job. If we hadn't come here at your request, I'd have been earning more pounds a week now than you are here, and don't you forget it."

"I'm not likely to forget it, the times you remind me."

"I had a letter from Bob this morning asking

me to go and do a modelling job for him next month."

"No you didn't. I read all your letters, and I'm telling you that if you go near that great fat slob again I'll knock your brains out."

"Did you say you read my letters?" I said with gathering momentum, knowing quite well that he did, just as he knew that I usually read his. "Did you say that you read my letters? Of all the mean, unspeakable things to do to anyone. You're not fit to live with; if it weren't for the children I'd leave you tomorrow."

"You can go," he said. "I wish to God you'd go, and take all your filthy rubbish with you," and with that he advanced on the small marble pillar, picked it up in his arms, staggered out to the door at the top of the stairs and hurled it down the stairs to the garage below. It made an extraordinary noise in its descent, and woke Joseph, who had been sleeping in his pram by the garage door. He started to cry, and David and I stared at each other at the top of the stairs in amazement. I hardly knew what to say: whether to comment on his feat of strength, whether to deplore his violence, whether to point out that the stairs had suffered damage or whether to walk out of the house. What I finally came out with was:

"You might have killed Joseph," which was quite untrue as the pram was well out of any direct line of attack from the staircase and the pillar had ended up a good three yards from him.

"What nonsense," said David righteously but quietly, and I went down to pick my baby up. On the way back up the stairs I put my foot

right through one of the floorboards: the pillar
had also destroyed the last few banisters and
the newel post. David seemed strangely ap-
peased by his action, and said to Pascal, who
had arrived in curlers to enquire what had happened:

"Oh, it's nothing, just a slight accident."
Flora, too, appeared, with a couple of curlers
in, and started to tell me about Daddy's hair-
cut. I left her with David and went to the telephone and rang up some men to come and fix
the stairs. I told them to come very urgently,
which they did, and the job cost us twelve
pounds. I said to David as he left for the theatre that evening:

"Well, we all have to pay for our own ex-
cesses, and at least I've got something left to
show for mine," and he replied:

"It's all very well if you do pay for your own,
you seem to forget that most of the time I pay
for yours as well."

That night, while David was out, Wyndham
rang. He was sorry he hadn't let me know he
was going, he was sorry he hadn't got in touch
with me before, he'd been in London discussing the next production with its author, Edmund Carpenter, and would I like to go out
with him the following Wednesday? I said no,
Wednesday was Pascal's day off. What about
Thursday? I said no, on Thursday I had a friend
coming round for the evening. What about Friday then? he said, and I agreed, as I could
hear that that was the last invitation that I was
going to receive.

We went to the restaurant that we had been

to before, and he told me some boring stories about Edmund Carpenter and his wife, and some interesting stories about his sister, who had married a very rich man and who could not forgive Wyndham for having made so much money on his own account, as she had once had visions of helping him along in his unsuccessful artistic career. I began to piece together, almost despite myself, his background: a father from a distinguished family, neither quite as wealthy nor quite as talented as he might have been, a mother longing for London in a style that she could not afford, a sister out to be able to afford anything and Wyndham wanting neither money nor hard work, but some kind of easygoing fame, which I thought he had well enough achieved. He had been born not exactly with a silver spoon, but with many other advantages. We were talking at one point about ambition, and I asked him what and how much he still wanted, and he said he was too lazy to take his profession seriously. I did not know whether this was the truth or an excuse. Then he said:

"I used to think, when I was younger, that nothing could be worse than wanting something and not getting it, something like greatness, or fame, or a knighthood, or a lead in a film, but I don't see things that way any more. The more I do, the more limitations I find in myself, the happier I am. I've got to like it, the warm cozy feeling of defeat."

It seemed improbable, this account of himself. I did not understand it, it did not appeal to me, but I remembered it.

We went to the same restaurant on the same

day the week afterwards, and he told me some
of the same stories and some different ones,
and remarked unfavourably on my habit of eating three plates of *hor d'oeuvres* instead of a
main dish.

"What you need," he said, "is a good red
steak. Most of you girls live on nice big steaks,
you're a bloodthirsty lot; no wonder you look
so colourless compared with all the rest."

We went there the week afterwards, too,
though on a different day of the week, and I
offended him on this occasion, I remember, by
asking him what he had come to Hereford for
in the first place.

"What do you mean?" he said indignantly. "I
think it's a perfectly useful thing to be doing,
don't you, opening a theatre here? Didn't you
read what I wrote in *Dramatic Events?*"

I assured him that I had read it and thought
highly of his concern for the cultural life of the
provinces, but could hardly believe that he was
naïve enough to believe that his good influence
would endure after his departure.

"Tell me why you think I came," he then
said, so I told him: I said that the only explanation I could find was that he wanted a rest from
the West End, that he wanted to be a big
fish in a small pond and to relax for a few
months in the heady atmosphere of artistic
gratitude. He was justifiably annoyed, and said
crossly:

"If you really want to know why I came, it's
because I used to like it round here so much
when I was a boy, I'm old enough now to
spend six months in the country for pure sentiment and old time's sake."

We went there the next week, too. Our liaison took on a certain regularity, and I grew used to telling lies to David and Pascal. But although it took on regularity, it did not exactly progress, or not in the one way that one might expect. The reluctance was wholly on my side, though there must have been something on his to make him put up with me: I simply could not bring myself to do it. Kissing I did not mind: in fact, I soon discovered that anything above the waist, so to speak, I did not mind, but anything below was out of the question, and after a few assays we reached a temporary truce. We were restrained, of course, by the secrecy involved: we could not meet during the daytime, and in the evenings we had to clear out of a ten-mile radius for fear of meeting people we knew. We did a good deal of driving round the countryside, but the car, though comfortable, was not all that comfortable. It soon became clear that Wyndham's aunt's house had been something in the way of a missed opportunity, but he had not had the keys and the grass had been wet.

We were experiencing, in fact, all the difficulties that beset young couples who live at home and have nowhere to go; and this for me increased the interest greatly. We could not go to Wyndham's flat as it adjoined the theatre and people were always likely to drop in, nor to my house because of the children and Pascal's habit of coming home early in tears in the middle of her evenings out, after quarrels with her boyfriend. We did once risk going to Wyndham's after our habitual excursion for dinner, and we had just settled on the settee when

the bell rang and Neville, Julian, the boy with
fanatic eyes and a girl I did not know all arrived and started to deliver some elaborate
complaint about what the house manager had
been saying to their relatives about getting
tickets. Wyndham told them it was nothing to
do with him and poured them all a drink,
which was more probably what they had come
for, and we sat round and tried to stop the
fanatic man from telling us about what was
going on with his soft palate and his epiglottis.
They did not seem unduly impressed by my
presence, and as far as I know, David never
learned about this particular instance.

It is quite clear, I suppose, to all that this
pace suited me far more than it suited Wyndham Farrar, men being what they are and
women being what they are said to be. He
would say as much from time to time. He
would make remarks like "I suppose we are going to make it some time, aren't we?" and
"We've only got three months of the season left,
you know." The first serious attempt which he
made to get things organized was about three
weeks after he had begun rehearsals for the
Carpenter play. He had a cold, and he told
everyone that he was going to bed for the
evening, as indeed I am sure he had every intention of doing, and that he was not to be
disturbed. He arranged for me to call on him,
carrying a parcel with a Boots label on.

"It's perfectly plausible," he said over the
phone, "for me to have asked you to buy me
some things, don't you think?"

It seemed ludicrous to me, the kind of idea
that David might have had, but I said nothing,

and called on him at the appointed hour, apparently unobserved. I found when I saw him that he really had got a cold.

"Hello," he said. "I thought we'd have a quiet evening at home. I just don't feel up to driving all round the bloody countryside."

"That's all right," I said, and so it might have been, but for a series of minor irritations which managed to put me off the idea altogether. First of all, he insisted on showing and explaining to me his model for the set of his next play. It meant less than nothing to me, for I could not even understand the terminology he used. David at least knew better than to talk to me of cycloramas and revolves. Then he asked me if I liked music, and without waiting for an answer put on some Wagner, and Wagner is the one composer about whom I have any feelings at all: he makes my blood run cold. Then he asked me if I would like some supper, and what about some bacon and eggs? Fine, I said, and then discovered that I had to cook them. I suppose that it would have been unlikely that I should have stood round and watched him do it, but nevertheless, the thought of myself in an apron asking him if he liked his eggs hard or soft or fried on both sides did not accord easily with my ideas of passion. And you may say, after a remark like that, do you still call yourself a practical woman? and I will say no, not perhaps that, but a factual one still, a factual one. We ate our bacon and eggs, listening to that thundering fascist, and he did not even offer me a drink. I began to suspect that perhaps he was one of those men who never drink when alone and enjoy nothing

more than putting their feet up. I thought that
if I had been Sophy I would have helped myself, but that being myself, I preferred the silent indictment of waiting. When we had finished eating, I took the plates back into the
kitchen. I was determined not to start washing
up, but the masculine squalor of the sink and
its surroundings compelled me. Nothing had
been touched since the morning before: the
sink hole was stopped with a mound of tea
leaves, and there was a pile of dirty cups and
saucers all over the draining-board. I looked
anxiously for a glass or two, but there were
none; my suspicions were right, he must be a
secret abstainer.

I had finished the washing up and was in
the middle of wiping the draining-board and
the kitchen table when he came to see what I
was doing.

"What on earth are you doing all that for?"
he said, and I replied:

"You forget, I don't like mess."

When I tore myself away from it, we went
and sat down on the settee and kissed in some
discomfort. After a while he said that perhaps
we might go up and lie on the bed, and I said
that perhaps we might, so we went up to the
bedroom. But it was useless, I could not bring
myself to think about it at all.

"What's the matter?" he said after a while.
"What's the matter with me? What have I
done? Don't you want me to make love to you,
Emma?"

"Not particularly," I said, turning over and
lying on my back to stare at the ceiling. "Not
particularly, to tell you the truth."

"Why not?"

"Oh, I don't know," I said. "All that washing up, and I can see that there's a button off your shirt, and I know that any minute now you're going to ask me to sew it on for you, aren't you? Be honest, tell me, you were, weren't you?"

"Well, it had crossed my mind. But not immediately, of course. Not now."

"No. After."

"Yes, I suppose so. After."

I started to laugh.

"Oh well," I said, "at least you admitted it. If you hadn't admitted it, that would have been that. Tell me, Wyndham, what makes you think that I'm any better at sewing buttons on than you are?"

"Well, you're a woman. More practice."

"You could start practicing now. Then you wouldn't have to take women to bed with you in order to get your buttons sewn on. I'll give you a lesson."

"Don't be so hard on me, Emma. I love you. For what that's worth."

"I don't even know what it means."

"It doesn't mean much. But it means something."

"I'm not really hard on you. I love you, too, in my own small way."

"Do you? Do you think about me?"

"When I've time. No, I really mean it, I do think about you. But I have other things to do. I'm not free. I would be loving you if I could manage it. Or I think I would."

"No you wouldn't. All you want is to be driven round in a nice big car and eat avocado pears and prawn cocktails and be stared at by men in provincial restaurants."

"Now you're being hard on me. And anyway, that's not all I want, I don't think it's all I want. It's just that I connect love—well, lying on beds and so forth—I connect that with babies. And being tired. And wanting to go to sleep. And I don't want all that, I just want to have a good time."

"But when you were a girl, Emma, you used to have a good time. You wouldn't have thought twice about a thing like this."

"I know I wouldn't. But I'm not a girl any more, am I?"

"You're not so old."

"No, I'm not so old."

"You do feel something for me, don't you?"

"Of course I do, I've told you I do. For God's sake, Wyndham, don't just lie there, smoke a cigarette or something. And light me one at the same time. Of course I feel something for you, sometimes I feel a terrible lot about you, but I'm just not equipped to deal with it, I'm in no position to deal with it, I haven't time for you. It's not fair on you, it's not what you want. I feel about you as I used to feel about the first boy I was ever in love with; he was an undergraduate at Cambridge while I was still a schoolgirl. I hardly knew him, but my father used to ask him to come to tea sometimes and I used to shake and tremble and watched the clock and hand round the sugar so that my hand might touch his when he picked up the sugar spoon. That's not love, that's craziness: I didn't know the man. I don't know you. I don't want to know you. I hate it when I see that your button's missing. I only know one person, and that's David, and I don't want to know anyone else. It's horrible, quite horrible, knowing people. But what do you want with this kind of crazy schoolgirl passion? It's no good for you, I can see it's no good for you. What you want is something nice and warm and lovely, like Sophy Brent."

"How very odd," he said, "that you should mention Sophy Brent. She was what I thought I was going to get when I fixed this season up. I had my eye on her from the start, I can tell you."

"I realized that. I'm sure it's not too late. Aren't you sorry now, that you got distracted?"

"I'm sure you didn't distract me on purpose."

"I didn't say no."

"I always get the sense that you're just about to."

"Do you? Are you sorry that you've got me on your hands rather than Sophy?"

"No, I'm not sorry. I can see that Sophy's nice and easy and straightforward, but you have your attractions, too. The attraction of the difficult. Trying to get a kiss out of you is like trying to get blood out of a stone. It makes me feel proud of myself when I get anything out of you."

"I don't mean to be difficult."

"Don't you? You don't do it on purpose, to keep me where you've got me?"

"Where have I got you?"

"Well, here."

"No. I don't do it on purpose. I can't see what you want me for. And that's the truth, for once."

"I want you because I think I still might get you. Or shouldn't I tell you that?"

"I still think I might get you, too. Though I'm beginning to doubt it."

"Anyway, I'm sure your conversation is more interesting than Sophy Brent's."

"I should bloody well hope so," I cried at this last humiliation, "but who's interested in conversation?" and I rolled over towards him, and we lay in each other's arms and gently kissed and suffered until it was time for me to go.

12

I DO NOT know quite how it happened, but after this encounter my halfhearted affair with Wyndham began to grow more and more public. What a useful word the word "affair" is, so abstract and nebulous, so like what actually happens. I do not know whether people started to talk, for it is certain that if they did it would not be me that they would talk to, but I gained a distinct impression of being watched. Wyndham was around a good deal, as he was busy working on the new play. I kept meeting him in the street, and I always felt that people could seize from distant windows the tone of our conjunctions. It is a small town, and there was an actor lodging in every

street. And every time I went near the theatre
I would come across Wyndham, and madman
Don Franklin once saw us embracing halfway
up the stairs to the dressing rooms. Although
this was not in itself decisive, as people are always embracing all over theatres for all sorts of
unloving reasons, I felt that it would get round.
Also, Wyndham carelessly rang twice in the
evenings after David had got back from work:
one time I answered, and had to explain that I
could not talk, and the other time Dave answered, and Wyndham had to ring off.

There were also two incidents that suggested that something at least, however vague,
was widely known. The first occurred one day
when I was out in the Festival Gardens with
Flora, feeding the ducks: there I encountered
Wyndham, who was walking up and down by
the river in conference with Edmund Carpenter. Wyndham introduced us, and instead of
walking on and leaving it at that they both
went to great lengths to amuse me and my
child. Edmund even bought Flora an ice cream
from the kiosk outside the theatre, and we all
sat on a park bench while she ate it. I was
touched and happy to be sitting there with
them and Flora together, worrying about no
absences, in the warm sun. And as we talked I
gathered a clear impression that Edmund had
heard about me already, for he treated me with
a mixture of deference and innuendo that
seemed to suggest prior information. When
Flora saw David at teatime that day, she talked
a good deal about ice cream and windows: it
took me some time to work out what the win-

dows referred to, and I don't think David ever got there.

The other incident took place while I was waiting for David by the stage door one evening: we were going out to dinner with a visiting friend who had come to see the show. I was reading the notices on the green baize noticeboard, and had just started on the understudy list for *The Maple Tree* when Julian appeared and greeted me.

"Hello," I said. "How are you these days? I haven't seen you for ages."

"I'm all right," said Julian, "I suppose. Have a fruit gum."

I accepted a fruit gum, and then said, wanting to talk and yet not being able to think of anything interesting:

"How's *The Maple Tree* coming along?"

"Oh, don't ask me," he said glumly. "I've no idea what the thing's about, I really haven't. I've only got two lines, anyway. Do you know what I say? I say, 'The general wishes you to know that he will not support any action involving horses,' and, 'Excuse me, madam, I think you must have lost this in the garden.' It's quite funny, really, I suppose."

"Have you got a nice understudy?" I asked, knowing that this was the next thing to say, and Julian brightened faintly.

"Its' not bad," he said. "I'm understudying Don again. I'm understudying him in every play, and he's never been off yet. He never will be off. He's as strong as a horse, and you should hear him going on all the time, you'd think he was dying. He's always getting his dresser to send messages along to me that he won't be able to go on, that I've got to be ready to take over at the interval, but nothing ever happens."

"Poor Julian. Still, it's not for so much longer, is it?"

"I don't know what I'll do when I leave here. I'll probably never get another job."

"That's what everyone says."

"I say, Emma, you don't happen to know what Wyndham's doing next, do you?"

"No, I've no idea."

"I just thought that if there was anything going you might mention me . . . they tell me that there's a good chance that one of these will transfer to London at the end of the season; it'd just be right, to go into town in the autumn. Have you heard anything about that?"

"I haven't heard a thing," I said stiffly, and Julian took the hint. He gave me another fruit gum and wandered off to change, but he left me thinking. It seemed that my life was no longer a dark secret, but had become the subject of speculation. I had a feeling that my affair with Wyndham Farrar would be known throughout the profession before it had even taken place.

But what was for me the final moment of exposure had nothing to do with the theatre: it arrived just before the first night of the Carpenter play. Wyndham could not work on it much in the evenings as most of his actors were playing every night, so he asked me if I would like to go out for a meal. He had to be back by ten, to go over a scene with Peter Yates, so we did not go as far afield as usual, but went to a place that he had heard of that was only seven miles out of town: another symptom, this, of

our growing carelessness. There was nobody
there that we knew, so we settled down to our
usual games with the menu and arguments
over the wine list. The odd monotony of our
outings had given us a highly sophisticated
knowledge of each other's appetites, so that
we behaved like an old married couple, and
warned each other off the shrimps or the potatoes with charming solicitude. This place,
however, was a little different from our usual
haunts: it was a huge barnlike building decorated with saddles and bridles and horse
brasses, and run by a jolly military man with a
moustache. There was nothing on the menu but
steak, and when the steak arrived it was the
hugest piece I have ever seen, and it tasted
distressingly of animal. I complained of this to
Wyndham, who said that it was the fault of my
feeble palate, which was accustomed only to
frozen meat. I said on the contrary, I had a
good palate, and that in my opinion, the
strange flavour was due to the fact that the bul-
lock we were eating had not been dead long
enough, and that freshly killed meat always
tasted odd. I went on to complain about the
predominance of butchers' shops in the area,
and Wyndham asked me if I had ever been to
the cattle market, and described it to me in
detail.

"I used to visit it," he said, "when I was a
boy," but I did not take him up on it. Instead, I
was reminded of my own visits to nearby Cheltenham as a child, and how we used to go
riding, as all middle-class girls go riding. We
talked about this a little, and why girls should
care so much more about horses than boys, and

so forth. We had finished our steaks by now, and were holding hands on the table and staring at each other. I had just remarked that it seemed strange that I should once have known such a load of irrelevant rubbish as the name of every piece of a horse's bridle, of every part of a horse's body and of every ailment to which a horse is subject: namely spavins, splints, glanders, megrim, colic and a whole lot more, when, detaching myself for an instant from Wyndham's ardent and exhaustive gaze, I happened to glance beyond him and caught sight, at a table behind him, of Mary Scott and her husband, Henry Summers. Or I assumed the man to be her husband; it was too much to hope that he was not.

I do not know what my face can have looked like as I registered their presence, but I felt myself blushing, and Wyndham immediately said:

"Now what's the matter, who've you seen now?"

"It's nobody," I said, "nobody that matters. Just an old school friend of mine."

"You'd better let go of my hand," he said, but I hung on to it all the tighter.

"They don't matter," I said.

"Where are they?"

"Behind you. Don't turn round and look."

"Don't you look at them either."

"I can't help it," I said, and tried to look down at the tablecloth.

"Who are they?" he said, and I tried to explain who Mary was and what she signified.

"I can't understand it," I said several times. "I can't understand what she's doing in a place

like this. It's such a lovely vulgar good-time
place, it's not her kind of place at all."

"But what does it matter?" he said when I
had told him all about her. "I don't see that it
matters, you're not in touch with her any
more."

"I know it doesn't matter," I said. "It's just
that she will be so shocked. And you see this
thing that I'm wearing, do you know what it
is?"

"What thing?"

"This pinafore dress affair."

"Well, what is it?"

"It's my old school gym slip, the one I had in
the sixth form. It seems so frightful, somehow,
so cheap and frightful, to be sitting here in a
place like this, wearing this."

Wyndham started to laugh.

"You are a joke," he said. "I thought you reminded me of something tonight. Do you know
what you remind me of? You remind me of a
head girl at a fashionable girls' school."

"That's just what Mary was," I said, hardly
knowing whether I was about to laugh myself
or not. "She was head girl, not me. I was a pre-
fect, but I wasn't head girl."

"What on earth are you wearing that thing
for?"

"I don't know. It just seemed smart, somehow. And it's such a lovely bottle green."

At this point I looked over towards Mary
again, and this time, as was inevitable, she
caught my eye. She smiled and waved, and
that was all there was to it. Though naturally
she had already taken everything in. On our
way out we had to walk past her table. I

paused for a moment, and she introduced her husband to me, and asked me how I was, and how the children were, and apologized for not having called to see me again.

"You must come and see us," she said, "but I expect that with the children you'll be very tied. Perhaps it would be easier for me to come across one day to see you."

"That would be lovely," I said. "Please do."

"I certainly shall," she said. "I'll just give you a ring and pop over one day, shall I? And perhaps you and your husband could come over to dinner one evening, do you think?"

"That would be lovely," I repeated, and smilingly departed. I knew that we would never meet again.

In the car I was gloomy and silent. After three or four miles Wyndham said, out of the silence, "You know, the trouble with you, Emma, is that you enjoy shocking your school friends more than you enjoy my company."

"Yes," I acknowledged gloomily, "that's the truth. That's what's the trouble with all of us. Cheap and vulgar, and all we want is attention. And what on earth is there to be done about that?"

It was by now the middle of July; the season was more than halfway over, and I realized one day as I walked towards the theatre to watch a dress rehearsal of *The Maple Tree* that when this new production had been launched there was no reason at all why Wyndham Farrar should remain in Hereford. A director does not usually hang around when he is no longer needed. There was nothing to prevent him from returning to London, that paradise of famous emotional girls. He had said nothing about any imminent departure, but it was suddenly obvious that he must at some point go. I almost wished he would: I could think of nothing pleasanter, during these days of clandestine pointlessness, than a return to my daily preoccupations with Flora and Joseph and the decor of my sitting room and Italian grammar. And during the dress rehearsal itself there was a peculiarly nasty moment, which increased my desire to be rid of the whole semi-interesting affair. Wyndham, who was not in the best of tempers, suddenly yelled from the front stalls at Julian, who was standing around looking helpless as usual:

"For God's sake, Julian, try to get a bit more attack into it, you look exactly like a frightened rabbit."

Julian flinched and said he was sorry, and went on looking just the same; but I walked out of the theatre, I was so horrified. It seemed to me to be the kind of thing that one just does not say to other people, the kind of physically wounding cruelty that is never forgiven.

I did not see Wyndham again before the first night. He rang once, but I said that I was too busy to talk, and put down the telephone. I did not want to go and see the show at all: I did not dislike the play, nor did I find it particularly interesting. It was about power, I think. Peter Yates played a dying king, and Natalie Winter and Sophy his mistress and his wife. David was the wife's lover. It was all most witty and abstract and philosophical, not a fact in the whole piece. Eventually, an hour before the thing was due to begin, I asked Pascal if she would like to go instead of me, and gave her my ticket, saying that I would stay at home. I told her, however, to come back at the end, as I thought I might go to the party. Edmund Carpenter himself was giving a party at one of the big hotels, and I did not feel strong enough to miss that. As I sat alone that evening, I thought about parties, and how I was always going to them, and how different they were from the kind of parties I used to enjoy at Cambridge: hard, bouncy parties, those ones at Cambridge used to be, where it would be important to say something new or bright, to be edgy and sharp and suspicious and concealed all at once. But these theatrical parties, I had never got my hand in with them: it was so important not to say anything new, so necessary to keep repeating the same old phrases, so vital to praise, at least in words, and so vital not to suspect. David, of course, did not do these things, for he is the rudest of the rude; but on the other hand, he is rude without finesse, without malice, with the same kind of exuberance that produces the darlings and wonderfuls and fantastics of the others.

I did not start to dress until Pascal got back, and by the time I got to the hotel people were already quite gay. Edmund met me at the door.

"Hello," he said. "I've had a few enquiries after you, where've you been?"

"I just didn't feel like going," I said, forgetting that he had written the play, and then, remembering it, "How did it go?" I asked.

"Oh, quite nicely, quite nicely," he said. "One mustn't expect too much, you know, with an intellectual piece. It'll probably transfer anyway, on the strength of Wyndham's name, don't you think? So long as the critics aren't too unkind, don't you think? Your friend Wyndham did quite a good job on it, if you ask me. All that business with the throne in the second act, that's all his, you know."

"Is it? I didn't quite get that bit."

"Neither did I, but it was very effective, don't you think?"

"Dramatically, you mean?"

"Well, yes, dramatically. I'm a bit out of touch with the theatre myself, you know, I've been writing film scripts for the last five years. There's a lot more money in it, you know, and all sorts of expenses. Why don't you get Wyndham to go in for films?"

"I thought he made a film once."

"Yes, he did. It wasn't a very good one. He should have stuck at it. I think it's a bit too serious for him, films, you know. He'd need talking into it."

"I'm not going to talk him into it."

"Why not? You'd make a very interesting *nouvelle vague* film star."

"I don't want to be a film star."

"I thought all actresses wanted to be film stars."

"I'm not an actress."

"Aren't you really? That's funny, I always thought you were. What do you do then?"

"It's hard to say," I said, trying not to sound sad. "It's really rather hard to say. I just try to keep myself in condition, that's all."

"In condition for what?"

"Oh, I don't know. Anything that should come along."

"What a funny girl you are. Why don't you go and find Wyndham? He was looking for you. I think he's in the cocktail bar. Go and get him to give you a cocktail."

"All right, I will," I said, and wandered on, asking myself in what way Wyndham could have talked to Edmund about me that could have entailed not saying that I was not an actress. What frightful things do men say to men about women, anyway?

I did not look for Wyndham or indeed for anyone. I drifted round, speaking to no one and moving on quickly when I saw David discussing with Don Franklin the problem of who had put his goblet down on the table slightly too far to the right in the drinking scene until I came up against Julian, who was sitting dolefully in a large chintz hotel chair, holding the hand of one of the youngest girls in the company, who looked almost as doleful as he did.

"Hello," I said, and he said "Hello," and patted the other arm of the chair, which I sat on. He then took my hand.

"How are you?" I said.

"Oh, surviving," he said glumly. "What about you? What did you think of this thing tonight?"

"I wasn't there."

"You weren't there? Lucky you. Quite a jolly little piece, don't you think? I don't think. Still, I hope it went all right, I hope it goes into the West End in September, or I'll be out of work again."

"You look a bit depressed," I said. I could hardly say less.

"I'm fed up with this place," said Julian. "It gets on your nerves after a bit, don't you find? Too like home. What on earth do you do with yourself, you're not even working?"

"I don't do much."

"Do you like it?"

"Not much."

"Everyone's scared to death of you, Emma. Did you know that? That's true, isn't it, Mavis?" he said, appealing to the limp girl holding his other hand, who started and said:

"Oh yes, of course, quite true."

"I don't much mind that," I said.

"I saw your lovely daughter yesterday. And you. You were down by the river, in the Festival Gardens, feeding the ducks. She's got a good overarm throw, your Flora."

"She has, hasn't she? Where did you see us from?"

"From my dressing room. You get a pretty good view from my dressing room window."

"I like it down there. I think we must have given the ducks indigestion yesterday: we hadn't any stale bread left so I had to buy a new loaf and cut a chunk off. I should think new bread would be frightfully bad for them, wouldn't you?"

"I should think they'll all swell up and die, poor things," said Julian.

After that we said nothing more. I sat there for another five minutes, until my eyes began to close and my head to nod with sleep. I then got up and released my hand from Julian's. He hardly registered my withdrawal, but continued to sit there, his face expressing sorrow worse than tears. It is strange, the public instinct for sorrow that will make a boy choose to sit and grieve in an armchair at a party in full view rather than alone in bed.

When I left Julian, Wyndham quickly caught up on me. I saw him coming, and tried to make my way through a door, but the door led only into a small sitting room, so I was trapped. He asked me what I had thought of the play, and I said that I had not been there; he asked me why not, and I said that I had not wanted to go. He was at his most unappealing: self-important, bullying, self-satisfied. I wondered how I could have been so foolish as to have been taken in, ever, by his line of talk, which he had admitted that he had been quite ready to try on Sophy Brent or any other girl in the place who would listen. We argued, in subdued tones, and after a few minutes I walked off, saying that I was going to look for David, to ask him to take me home. But I could not find David anywhere. I looked all over the ground floor of the hotel, which was dedicated to merriment, and even went upstairs to see if he was sitting round up there. When I got there I did sit round a little myself: it was so removed and quiet, and the vast areas of red carpet were soothing. There were also some nice oil paintings of bulls, which I much admired, and a huge gilt-framed mirror, which I would not have minded having. While I sat there, a real live resident came out of his bedroom and crossed the corridor to go to the bathroom; he was wearing a maroon silk dressing gown, and he tiptoed in his bedroom slippers, as though

afraid of disturbing the noise below. I felt it
was rude in some way to sit there on the land-
ing chair until he came out, but I remained,
and when he emerged he nodded at me shyly
and said, "Good night."

Later I went down again. There was still no
sign of David, so I thought I would go home,
and I was just about to slip out quickly when
Edmund Carpenter got hold of me just by the
door. He was a conscientious host, and had
been by the door all evening. I had to stay
and thank him and talk to him and wish him
luck with his reviews. He seemed to wish to
embark once more upon profundities, and
asked me what I thought of a man who wanted
to write great plays and spent his time writing
films in warm climates. I was racking my brain
for some opinion when Wyndham appeared.

"Oh, just on your way home," he said, seeing
me. "I'll walk you back."

"That's right," said Edmund, "you walk her
home."

I stared at their two more or less middle-
aged faces and admitted defeat.

"Where's your coat?" said Wyndham.

"I didn't bring a coat," I said, and walked
out through the front door, where a man in
white nodded and bowed and scraped.

"You're a silly child," said Wyndham. "It's a
cold night, you can't possibly walk home in
that thing."

"I don't see how you're going to stop me," I
said, and walked off briskly down the back
street that led directly to my house. He followed me, and caught up and took me by the
elbow.

"It's ridiculous," he said, digging his fingers into me hard, "you'll catch your death of cold."

"Don't treat me like a child," I said. "I'm not a child."

"You behave like a child. How do you expect to be treated?"

"With a little human dignity," I said.

"Human dignity," he repeated, "human dignity. You don't know what it is. You treat me like a fool, you eat my food, you drink my drink, you take my presents off me and you treat me like a fool. And then you talk about human dignity. You're a child, I'm telling you, you think you can take everything and give nothing."

"Well, if I think that, I think it. There's no altering me."

"What's so wonderful about you that you shouldn't be altered?"

I was shivering by now, like an idiot: the cold night air had overcome the heat which I had carried with me from the stuffy hotel, and was embracing me damply inside my thin linen dress. I did not listen to what Wyndham was saying: I hurried on, trying to get back to bed. When I reached the front of our house, I got out my Yale key and unlocked our front door and turned round to say good-bye:

"Good night, and clear off and leave me alone," was what I in fact said, in an angry whisper, for I was afraid that David might be lying awake in bed and listening for my return.

"You realize," Wyndham said, "that I won't be staying in this place much longer? I've got a few things to tidy up, and then that's it."

"Well, if that's it, that's it," I said, "and a pretty fruitless business it's been," and I stepped into the garage. I tried to shut the door in his face, but he took hold of it and pushed it in and stepped in after me, and was just about to grab hold of me when I heard a scuffle and clatter behind me. I spun round to see what it could be: the light was very poor, but both Wyndham and I could easily distinguish David and Sophy, who had been lying on the packing cases at the bottom of the stairs. Sophy had jumped to her feet, and the noise we had heard had been David, who had put his foot through one of the packing cases and was trying to get himself loose. Sophy was trying to pull up and zip the top of her dress: I could see the smooth gleam of her shoulders. We all four stood and stared at one another. I was furious that David should be so mixed up with a lot of splintered wood, and I had not much time to think of anything else. David was the first to speak.

"I thought you were upstairs, Emma," he said. "I looked for you at the party, but you'd gone."

"I thought you were upstairs," I said. "I looked for you at the party, but you'd gone."

"I didn't expect you would be coming in here," he said.

"I didn't expect—" I said, and broke off, for I did not quite know what I had not expected.

Nobody said anything for some time, and then David helped Sophy to do up the back of her dress and Wyndham put his hand on my shoulder, expressing something—regret, pity, affection, something of that kind. I remember looking at Sophy's face, and even in a real situation I saw she could not act: her ripe and tender features expressed nothing, nothing at all, they were wiped of significance by the event, blank in meaningless surprise. I saw that nobody would do anything, so with immense snappy effort I pulled myself together and said in my brisk credible tones:

"Well, don't let's all stand here catching our deaths of cold. I'm going up to bed now, and I don't care which of you takes Sophy home, but I think somebody should set out at once," and I started off up the stairs. My words produced a subdued chorus from all three of them of "Are you all right, Emma?" and "You're sure you're feeling all right?" I ignored them, and went straight on and into my bedroom, where the first thing I did was to switch on the electric fire. I knew that it would be David who would come up to me, though perhaps it would have been more reasonable for Wyndham to have come. I was sitting in front of the fire trying to get warm when David appeared.

"Have they gone?" I said.

"Yes, they've gone," said David, beginning to get undressed. I, too, got undressed: silently climbed into bed and lay there, propped up rigid on the pillows. David got into bed, too, and turned off the light. I could not believe that neither of us was going to speak, but we were both asleep before we had made up our minds to do so.

The next day, as I got breakfast and washed up and made the bed, I thought about it all. It had been quite clear from their faces that David and Sophy had not been indulging in some

momentary after-party fling: what I had seen
had been going on as regularly and probably
more thoroughly than what they had seen between me and Wyndham. Now I knew it, other
things seemed to fit: of course, Sophy had always been round, but it had not been me she
had wanted, it had been David. And her visits
had presumably slacked off a little because she
had got him. I had been completely disarmed
by the bluntness of her admiration for him: all
those remarks about "Where's your lovely husband?" had seemed to me as meaningless as
anything else that came out of her lovely
mouth. I had had no suspicions at all, of
either of them, and I do not think I am credu-
lous or gullible. I could not get my mind round
it; I could understand that Sophy should want
him, but not that he should want her. He had
always before been so rude about stupidity and
bad acting, and Sophy was exactly the type of
professional seductress who usually arouses his
contempt. Nobody else took her seriously, so
why should he? I had not taken her seriously
myself: I had condescended to her, I had de-
fended her when others like Julian or Neville or
Viola had laughed at her, I had thought I had
been the only person round who could appreciate her peculiar brand of mindless instinctive
charm. I remembered the times I had spoken
up in praise of her, and how David on these
occasions had said nothing; and I could see
now that there had been something factitious
and self-willed in my praise. Her continual
hanging round had appealed to my vanity, and
because I had thought she was negligible and

harmless I had been prepared to see the best in her.

I saw that I would now have to reassess her. She was not harmless, there was something more there than I had thought. I wondered how far it could be possible that her sheer physical beauty had done it: I have always found it hard to believe that a man can love a woman despite her identity, and solely for eyes and thighs, and so forth. But then there was I myself, in a considerable state about Wyndham, whom I neither knew nor understood, whose identity had concerned me not at all: to me he had been little more than a dangerous high-powered object, like his own fast car or the deep dark brown floodwater river.

David went out that morning; he went out without saying a word. It crossed my mind that perhaps we would never speak to each other again, but would live together for the years to come in total silence. I knew such things had happened. I tried to keep myself busy, in order not to notice the depth of my horror, but from time to time I caught a glimpse of myself in the mirror, and my pale and blotchy features stared back at me with ridicule. And I knew then, for the first time, how much of a freak I truly was: in any other century but our own I would have been truly negligible, an unattractive, dark-skinned, spiky misfit, who would never have married, and who could at the best have hoped to be a bluestocking or a pillar of the Church. Whereas Sophy Brent was in with it by nature, she was on the side of all the flowering greenery, she was built for liaison and fruition, for passion, affection and infidelity. She would have been all right anywhere, in any age; and I had tried to pity her. I could not bear to think of my inferiority to such a girl.

We had lamb stew for lunch, and David did not come back. Flora kept saying, "Where's Daddy?" and I winced each time, as though he had really left me. I watched her in her high chair and wondered what I would do if I had to deal with her by myself, on a weekly allowance. This was what I had asked for in marrying David and in saying a qualified yes to Wyndham; this insecurity. But this time I was its victim, not its agent.

Pascal went out immediately after lunch, to her English course. When she had gone and I was almost alone, I sat down on the kitchen chair and started to cry. I cry so rarely that I was frightened: I sat there shaking and gasping, and wondering how to stop myself. Flora, who had been playing in the sitting room, came to see what I was doing, and when she arrived I attempted to pull myself together: I got up and thought I would make myself a cup of coffee, and put the milk in the pan. When I lit the match I broke my nail on the matchbox. Then I went to the 'fridge to put the milk bottle back, and I did not look where I was going, for I fell over one of Flora's bricks. I dropped the bottle, and it broke and splintered all over the floor. At the sight of it, and forgetting Flora, I started to cry all over again. She came stumbling towards me, through the broken glass and dirty milk, and threw her arms round my knees.

"No crying, Mummy, no crying," she said several times, then started to cry in sympathy.

"It's all right, Flora," I kept repeating as I

unclasped her hands and started to pick up the
lumps of glass. I persuaded her to sit down
while I tried to wipe up the milk with the floor
cloth. There was nearly a whole pint on the
floor, and I had to wring the cloth out several
times in the sink, and I had not thought that
there would be splinters of glass in the cloth. I
cut my hands and they started to bleed. I was
wearing sandals and no stockings, and my feet
were wet with milk: I can remember now the
slimy feeling of my feet on the leather soles. I
was overcome, submerged by such petty inlets
of defeat. I fight so hard against domestic
chaos, my efficiency is nothing but a reflection
of terror, and I stood there and rammed my
fists into my eyes and wept, and varied colours
came and went, blue and yellow and dilating
red, the flowers of grief, and I was damp with
milk and blood and tears, a varied sea of
grief.

It was Flora who brought me round. She
clung to me, whimpering and sobbing. When
my head cleared, I bent down and picked her
up, and she drew her arms around my neck
and kissed me and tried to wipe my face, saying:

"Better now, Mummy, better now."

But for her I would have been there still.
And because of her I kissed her back and said:

"Yes, better now, silly Mummy," and went
into the bathroom and washed my face and my
feet and combed my hair. I tried to think of
some way of spending the afternoon, for there
are a limited number of things that one can do
with two children, and decided I would go to
the launderette with all the things that I never

bother to wash in the machine at home, like bedspreads and dressing gowns. It would at least amuse Flora: she loves the launderette. So I carried everything downstairs and put it in the end of Joseph's pram, and the three of us set off.

I left Joe outside when we got there, and took Flora in with me. She insisted on putting all the clothes in the machine for me, although they were far too big and heavy for her, and I had to organize my help so that she did not notice I was helping. Such disciplines on another's behalf are perhaps some kind of salvation. Then I sat down and started to slip through one of the provided magazines, while Flora ran up and down peering through the portholes and screaming with delight at the sight of the swirling masses of fabric. I, too, was cheered by the presence of so much quiet mechanical activity, and by her intense enjoyment. I felt at home, almost as though I were in London.

As I sat there, a girl that I knew passed me with her basket, a square, worried-looking girl, who was married to one of the walk-ons. I smiled at her, and she stopped for a moment to chat. I was surprised, as people do not usually chat with me. At first I could not understand what she was talking about; she said something about the washing at home getting her down, and two and ninepence being an awful lot of money, but then at least it got a bit dry in the spinner and she didn't have to have the fire on so much at home to dry it off. I listened and agreed, but it was only when she had gone that I realized that she had been apologizing to me

for being there at all, that the launderette was
not to her a place of duty but a place of lazy,
extravagant luxury which she could not afford
to visit. She had been embarrassed, as though I
had caught her having her hair done at an expensive hairdresser's or eating cream cakes
alone in a tea shop.

When she left me, I looked round for Flora,
to give her the treat of putting in my second
instalment of soap powder, and I saw the back
view of somebody else that I knew. It was Sophy Brent, who was just shutting the door of
her machine. I stared at her: the well-cut
brown dress, the thick springing black hair, the
long brown legs, the lovely ripe extensions of
her, and as I stared Flora caught sight of her,
too, and rushed up to her, saying, "Sofa, Sofa."
Sophy turned, and I almost felt sorry for her as
she took in this knee-level approach. It is to
her everlasting credit that she managed to
smile and say, "Why, Flora, how lovely to see
you."

"Hello, Sophy," I said as she looked up at
me. Her face looked subdued and even a little
pale under its tan. "Hello, Emma," she replied,
and we stared at each other. Then I said as
the remark rose in my mind, "Do you come here
often?" and she said, "Quite often," as her machine started to whirr and hum.

"I come here," she added, "when I've nothing
better to do," and I suddenly thought, Then
where, oh where, is David? The query made me
feel a whole lot better, and I advanced on her
a little.

"I hope you got home all right," I said. "Did
Wyndham see you home?"

"Oh yes," she said. "I got home."

"I thought he would see you home all right," I said, and we continued to look at each other, finding nothing to say. Real conflict, for me at least, always turns out to be wordless, which is why I find drama and the theatre so unreal. We conflict because we cannot communicate, because there is nothing to be said. I know that realism is not all, but to me it is all, and anything that does not seem to be dredged up from a fleshy occurrence leaves me undisturbed. Symbols and images, oh yes, I have heard of them. But Sophy and I were there in the flesh, and though the implications might have been manifold the fact was one, and it was unaccompanied at the time by much discussion. I know what I am through her eyes: dark, bad-tempered, censorious, snobbish, and with all that quite ominously smart. And that was all I had to confront her with amongst those spinning white windows.

It was Flora who diverted us: she had wandered over to the door, and now came rushing back to tell me that Joe was crying. As I was free to leave my machine for the next twenty minutes, I thought I had better go and push him round. I said as much to Sophy, who said good-bye, and then, as I started off towards the door, followed me with:

"Wyndham told me he's leaving at the weekend, he said he was going to start work on a film. Do you know what it's going to be about?"

I immediately assumed that this was said to hurt me and to reveal my ignorance, but I was wrong, for she then remarked, without pausing and seemingly at a tangent, that she had had two rather good reviews that morning for her role in *The Maple Tree*. I said that I was delighted, but this was not the point: the point was that she hoped that Wyndham's opinion of her talent might have improved sufficiently for him to make her into a film star, and she was even prepared to try me, at such a moment, to see if there was anything in it for her. It was not my ignorance that she had assumed, but my complicity.

I left her, amazed as ever by this curious professional characteristic, and pushed Joe round to quieten him whilst I bought a few things. When the time came to pick up my washing, I found myself flinching from revisiting the launderette, for I could not be sure that Sophy would have had the sense to clear out while her machine went on its own automatic way. I wondered what happened to washing that nobody collected; presumably the attendant would remove it eventually and leave it to rot damply in a basket for some legal limited time, like three months. I did not like to think of such a fate being inflicted upon my bedspread because of Sophy Brent, so I returned and got my things back. Sophy had in fact gone, temporarily. I glanced into her porthole as I passed and noticed with absurd delighted malice that something she had put in had run, and dyed her whole wash a horrid muddy pink.

When I got out again and dumped the bag on Joe's feet, Flora started to suggest that we might go and see the ducks. The sky was the colour of damp slate, and seemed to be presenting a solid wall like a backcloth behind the farthest row of buildings, but as I have said, I cannot deny Flora much, and I thought that the pleasure it gave me to see her small face brighten into serious joy as we set out across the bridge to the riverside gardens would compensate for any amount of rain. When we got there, I gave Flora half of one of the buns I had bought for tea and watched her throw it in, and the greedy quarrels of the birds as they snapped and fought for each piece. I was wondering what I had done to David, what he had done to me and who had done it first, whether he had picked up Sophy because Wyndham had left her for him by preferring me or whether on the contrary, Wyndham had taken me because Sophy was already attached to David and thus not available, and whether the situation was in any way recuperable, whether David and I and Flora and Joseph would ever stand together by the water's edge again lobbing crumbs and possessed again by quiet discontented pleasure. I was wondering about all this when, as I leaned dreamily on the pram handle, I saw Wyndham approaching me from the other end, the theatre end, of the gardens. He was alone, and he was looking for me heavily, bearlike. I stood and waited: encumbered by two children, I had no choice. When he got near, I could see he was in a very bad temper. The first words he said were:

"What on earth did you mean by making me take that wretched girl home last night? I suppose you and David got into your snug little bed and had a merry old laugh at my expense, didn't you?"

"Do you really think so?" I said. Now I confronted him again I felt an immense lassitude;

I could hardly be bothered to feel, sensation involving such mess.

"What can I be expected to think?" he said moodily, staring at Joseph. "What am I supposed to think?" He seemed so angry that I could see why people got frightened of him at rehearsals.

"I don't know," I said. "And don't shout, you'll frighten the babies."

"Oh Christ," said Wyndham, "do you have to bring that lot with you wherever you go?"

"What do you mean?" I said. "They're my children, I want them with me, I love them."

"They're just about all you do seem to love," he said with some predictability. "You never think about anything but them. I don't know why your husband puts up with you, but I'm quite certain that I can't be expected to. You never give me more than a quarter of your attention at once, do you?"

"My husband doesn't put up with me," I said wearily, sinking more and more heavily on to the pram handle. "He prefers Sophy Brent."

"Oh, that can't be serious," he said. "That's just one of those things that happen. I daresay it's all your own fault anyway, refusing to sleep with anyone, even him, and he's a right to it. I knew that there was something wrong with you from the first, when you kept eating all those avocado pears and prawn cocktails and artichokes."

At this moment I happened to glance away from him, on one of those mechanical, half-conscious tours of the eye which check up on the safety of children. And I was just in time to catch sight of Flora as she slid from the extreme muddy edge of the bank into the water. I have seen this happen so often in imagination, have prepared for it so thoroughly in my fears, that I did not have to waste time in wonder: I was into the water with her as soon as she hit it, and just as it closed over her head. I saw her face go under as I was within an arm's length of her, and I saw her astonished eyes open under the water. It was not deep, but the bank shelved steeply, and everything I had ever heard about the treacherousness of the sylvan Wye rushed into my head as I grabbed her by a leg and hauled her towards me. I pulled her up into my arms, and then lost my footing myself, so that we were both floundering, with water up to my shoulders. I managed to hold her up as I groped for support, and in a moment I was sitting with her on the bank. She had started at last to cry, and I sat there, my feet still dangling in the weeds, trying to clasp her and keep her warm and comfort her, as she yelled and clutched and burrowed her damp head into my breasts. It did not cross my mind for some time to look around for help, and only when her crying had slacked off a little did I try to get right up the bank. When I turned, I saw Wyndham and a whole crowd of people who had collected to watch my ascent.

I struggled to my feet, and holding Flora firmly in one arm, stretched out the other to Wyndham, who pulled me up the remaining two feet of slope. I was immediately surrounded by a crowd of muttering, quiet well-wishers, too timid in their English fashion to interfere, but too curious and censorious to leave. I stood there dripping, my clothes clinging to me, every stitch and bone and knob of me exposed. If ever I have wished for the spectacular, I had it then. I remember that Wyndham took my arm, my free arm, and started to kiss my cheek, and then to tell everyone to go away, we could go to the theatre and get dry.

"Oh, she's from the theatre," one old woman said as though that accounted for it, as though I were some publicity stunt, but I was too far gone to care. The only thing I said was Joseph, where's Joseph, and Wyndham, decent, human old Wyndham, walked me back to the theatre, with one arm round me and the other pushing Joe and the washing in the pram. By the time we got to the theatre, Flora's screams had faded into moans.

"You'd better come into my house and get dry," Wyndham said, but I said that everyone was watching, and that I would rather go into the theatre and borrow Dave's towels and things in his dressing room. So he took me into the dressing room, leaving Joe with the doorkeeper, and I undressed Flora and dried her on David's towel and wrapped her up in one of the pram blankets. Then I undressed myself and put on David's dressing gown, as best I could with Flora in my arms, for she would not let me put her down for an instant. My memories are confused. I recollect the noise of her sobbing, and wet heaps of clothes, and my thanking Wyndham again and again, I am not sure for what, unless it was for pushing Joseph's pram for me.

Eventually I was free of the wetness and had time to try telling Flora that she was better now

and that she had been for a little swim with
Mummy, like the seaside. Wyndham said he
would take us home in the car, and when I
said I couldn't go home in a dressing gown
in his car he went off to the girls' dressing room
and returned with the only outdoor garment
he had found there, which happened to be a
mackintosh of Sophy Brent's. I put it on, worrying vaguely that both Flora and Wyndham
could see me naked at the same time, which
did not seem right, and then we went down to
the stage door to get Joseph. A crowd had already collected there, and Wyndham left me
to them as he went to bring his car round to the
door. Viola was there, and Julian. I think it was
Julian that got Joe out of his pram at the last
moment and handed him to me as I sat there
in the back of the car, acutely conscious of my
cold, bare thighs on that girl's cold mac.

Wyndham carried Joseph up the stairs when
we got back to the house, and there I found
David waiting for us. When Flora saw him she
screamed, "Daddy, Daddy," and held out her
arms to him. He took her, and I collapsed on to
the sofa and told him in a few brief words what
he could not already see. Flora seemed quiet-
ened by David; she even spoke to him. When he
asked her what she had been doing, she said,
"Ducks," and then she started to yell once
more, "Water, water," whereupon both David
and I, to stop her getting into her full vocal
stride, said simultaneously, and in almost exactly the same words,

"What a clever girl; fancy going for a swim
with your clothes on."

The thought arrested and distracted her, and the terrifying unison of our response made David and me exchange a look of awestruck fright. Wyndham meanwhile put Joseph down in an armchair and quietly departed.

David took Flora and dressed her, and I dressed myself. I was as deeply shocked by the fact that David and I had said the same thing at once as by anything else that had happened over the last couple of days. It seemed to indicate a knowledge shared with him that was so great that it excluded either the possibility of a future or the possibility of an end, and I did not know which. That rocky landscape that I had foreseen had now become a water's edge with ducks and mud, and I could not tell if it was in me to patrol the bank for the rest of my life.

David and I still said nothing to each other, for we spent what remained of the afternoon in trying to be nice to Flora and in trying to belittle the horrible experience she had undergone. We joked with her, and played with her, and drew her pictures of ducks and boats on the water, and presented to her a united front of comfort. I started to sing to her, which she always enjoys, but the song that kept coming into my head was this:

> Mother, may I go out to swim,
> O yes, my darling daughter,
> O yes, you may go out to swim,
> But don't go near the water.
>
> O mother, may I go out to swim,
> O yes, my darling daughter,
> But mind the boys don't see you get in,
> Keep right under the water.

I could not very well sing it, but it seemed appropriate to something: to marriage, perhaps, or the emancipation of women.

David had to leave for the theatre before Flora was in bed, so we did not have time to say anything to each other, but he did remark, as he put his head round the bathroom door as I was bathing her:

"You'd better go to bed early, Emma, you don't look too good."

I did not feel too good, either. I had a headache and a sore throat, and I went to bed at eight o'clock with some lemon and honey. I was asleep when he came in, and when I woke up in the morning I was so full of cold that I could hardly breathe. I got up, but felt so odd on my feet that I took my temperature, and upon finding that it was a hundred point four went straight back to bed again. So once more David and I had something to discuss other than our infidelities, and we jumped on it with alacrity. He wanted to send for a doctor, and I said that I did not want a doctor, and so on and so forth. He is always very solicitous whenever I am ill, especially when it is anything that might affect my lungs: although there is every indication to the contrary, he still believes that my mother's tendency to tuberculosis is likely to flourish at any moment. I do not blame him for worrying: a life of discipline like that my father led would hardly suit him.

I told him to take Flora off my hands as I did not want her to catch my cold, so he took her out, and Pascal looked after Joe. I slept for most of the day. I was surprised by how exhausted I felt, once I had, for the good of others, a reason to get out of the way and into bed. At teatime David came up to see me; he was carrying a huge parcel, and I thought for a moment that it must be for me, but he put it down on the bed and said:

"This is for Flora. I met Julian in town and he said he'd bought it for her. Isn't that nice of him? I don't know what it is, I thought I'd better let you unwrap it in case it's something hideously unsuitable, like plasticine."

"From Julian?" I said, amazed. "Why on earth from Julian?" and I started to undo the smooth brown wrappings. It was an enormous doll, one of those that walks and talks and eats and has real brushable hair; it was nearly as large as Flora herself, and it had several complete changes of clothes, with hats and gloves and shoes and socks and a lace parasol. I was overcome: I stared at the bright waxen cheeks and the black curls and the blue china rolling eyes and the long false lashes, the expensive, vulgar, brash beauty of it, and I felt that I was going to cry.

"What did he do it for?" I said, sniffing and trying to blow my nose. "Whatever did he do it for? Why should he give her a beautiful thing like this? Did he say anything to you when he saw you?"

"You think it's beautiful, do you?" said David, who had been staring at it in silence. "I think it's the horridest thing I've ever seen."

"I think it's lovely," I said. "I've never seen anything so lovely. What did Julian say?"

"Nothing very much. He just muttered something about having seen it in a shop, and wanting an excuse to buy it, and would I give it to you for Flora, to cheer her up after yesterday."

"I can't possibly give it her, can I? She'd ruin it in a moment, she wouldn't know what to do with it. Where is she now? Is she having tea?"

"Yes, she's having tea with the others."

"How's she been today? Has she mentioned it at all?"

"No, she hasn't said anything, but she wouldn't go near the river or the theatre; whenever we got anywhere near the bridge, her lip started to quiver and she started to say, 'Flora dry now,' so I kept well away."

"She didn't say anything about the ducks?"

"Oh, that was rather awful—she started to say 'Ducks,' and then she suddenly remembered and said, 'No ducks, no ducks,' over and over again. Poor kid."

"Oh, Dave, how frightful. Do you think she'll forget? She's little enough, she will forget, won't she?"

"Oh, she'll forget in no time. Don't worry about her."

"What will we do, David, what will we do when she reaches the age when she cries alone in her bed? Just crying, not crying for attention; you know what I mean. When I put her to bed last night I listened outside her door, and she went to bed quite cheerfully, and there wasn't a sound, and I thought that one day she'd be crying away in there, but quietly, so that we shouldn't hear, on purpose so that we shouldn't hear. I couldn't bear it, I don't think I could bear it."

"We don't think we can bear anything," said David, "until it happens." He started to wrap

the doll up again in its box, and then he suddenly said, as though we were pursuing some
abandoned conversation, "Anyway, why the
hell did you have to pick a man like Wyndham
Farrar?"

"What do you mean?" I said.

"Well," said David astonishingly, "you might
have chosen somebody who had nothing to
do with the theatre, you might have had an
affair with someone like Mike Papini. I could
see what he was after last time all right, but
you had to go and choose somebody right
under my bloody nose, somebody who at the
moment has my career in his hands, which
was a bloody silly thing to do, don't you think?
The whole profession must know about it by
now. You know what gossips they are, it'll be
all over London."

"I didn't look at it that way," I said, starting
falsely to laugh. "And you didn't go so far away
yourself, did you? What about Sophy Brent? If
she wasn't under your nose and mine, I'd like
to know who was. The times I've put up with
her pinching my cigarettes, through Christian
charity. I don't mind carrying on with the
Christian charity now, but don't expect me to
think you've made a brilliant choice, will you?
Fancy having an affair with the girl you're
playing opposite, I've never heard of anything
as corny as that. I suppose she threw herself
at you, as they say."

"I expected this last remark to annoy him,
but all he said was, smugly:

"Yes. I suppose you could say she did," and
then we were interrupted by Flora, who came

banging on the door, crying, "See Mummy, see Mummy," so that we had to let her in.

I took my temperature again later in the evening, when David had gone, and found that it had gone up by point two degrees, which made me feel more unwell than ever. I took some codeine and some hot whisky and at nine o'clock fell asleep. I dreamed, seemingly all night, of Julian. It was an extraordinary dream, clearer than some of life itself. We were walking through Islington, Julian and I and we were passionately in love. Islington itself was not the place I know it to be, but the place it must once have been, with wide grass walks and fields and dandelions growing in the paving stones. It was as green as it now is stony, and I felt for Julian all that I had ever felt for anyone. I can remember it so distinctly, that image of breathless, exhausting, total admiring love. We had our arms round each other, and I could even imagine in my dream what his thin girl's body would feel like to hold, so different from Wyndham's solid trunk or David's muscular torso; we were walking northwards from the Angel, towards Islington Green, and when we got there we sat down on one of the benches that bears the inscription "Persons are not allowed to sleep on this seat," and there we froze together in some immobile trance amongst the buttercups and meadowsweet. It was like a scene out of a book, a passion out of a poem, it had all the pure intensity that never occurs in life, the dizzy undistractedness, with no rivers, no children; so that when I woke I really felt that I had been elsewhere.

I also felt when I woke that it was time I

called the doctor. I got David to ring for me, and then lay there and waited. The doctor, when he arrived, was an authoritative-looking old man with white hair and a distinguished manner. He examined me all over and asked me if I was run-down and whether I had adequate help with the children. I said that I had, and he said that I didn't seem in too good a condition and that I ought to have a good rest. Yes, I said, that's all very well, I know my soul's in a bad way, but what about my nose and my throat? He laughed, and said that they weren't too bad, he would prescribe me some drops and some penicillin.

"The back of your throat looks soggy," he said.

I did not like the sound of that at all: I like doctors to use clinical, incomprehensible words, not descriptive laymen's words, like soggy. I could picture all too well the back of my throat. Then he said that he wasn't worried about my cold, that was nothing, but that I seemed to be run-down; the words run-down were, I thought, emotive rather than clinical, but I did not protest. He said that I should stay in bed and not worry about anything.

"I'll tell you what I'll do," he said. "I'll tell your husband and your *au pair* girl just to leave you alone, to go out somewhere and leave you alone. You can get up and get yourself something to eat; that won't do you as much harm as having them running in and out all day long. I know what families are like; they never give you a moment's peace, do they? You can drop dead and they still expect you to come to life again in time to get their breakfast."

I tried to suggest that in our family this was not exactly the case, but he would not listen.

"It's all very well," he said, "I know you've got a girl to help you, but let's face it, they can't do very much for you, can they? You say you were feeding the baby yourself until three months ago. Now that's a job that not many mothers will do these days. Don't tell me you wouldn't like a nice day in bed, with nobody in the house to bother you."

I was glad that he was so determined to be indulgent: his professional assessment of my need comforted me tremendously, and I began to see myself as a worn-out, legitimately exhausted housewife. When he left I relapsed into my pillows with a sigh, and when, a little later, David appeared and said that he had borrowed Neville's car and would take Pascal and the children out for the day as soon as Pascal came back with my prescriptions, I really began to fancy that I might indulge myself in a mild breakdown. I would opt out of it all, love and family and infidelity, and I would be ill. After they had gone I lay there dozing and sniffing the morning away. I realized of whom the doctor had reminded me: he had reminded me of my father, with his perennial willingness to believe the best of me. He had not expected much of me, that doctor: he had not expected too much of my body, as my father had never expected anything of my soul. They were two professionals, those two old men, and I lay back weakly, resting on their superior opinions of human limitation.

At about half past two, just as I was thinking of getting up to see what David had left me for lunch, the telephone rang. I rushed to answer it, and sure enough, it was Wyndham Farrar.

"Emma? How are you, Emma?" he said as soon as I lifted the receiver. "I hear you're very ill."

"I'm not at all ill," I said. "Who told you I was? I've just got a bad cold, that's all."

"I've been worrying about you."

"Have you? Then you might have rung yesterday."

"I didn't want to risk talking to David."

"Who told you David was out now?"

"Neville. They've gone out for the day in Neville's car. I know all about that. It's a small world. How's Flora?"

"Oh, she's all right. As far as the eye can see. Not that the eye can see very far."

"Emma, I'm coming over to see you."

"Oh, are you?"

"What can I bring you? Have you got enough to read?"

"Not really. But then I wouldn't want to read anything that you might have lying around, would I? The life of Mrs. Siddons, and all that rubbish?"

"I could go and get you something."

"Yes, you could, but please don't bother."

"I'll be straight round."

"All right," I said, and rang off.

I went straight back into the bedroom and looked at myself in the mirror. I looked pale, but thickly pale, not with the gravity of health, and my hair was a shaggy mess. I pulled a comb through it, and then started to look for my one never used lipstick. I put some on, and was startled by the eccentricity of the effect. It made me look a whole lot better, quite a different colour altogether, and but for the bleariness round my eyes and the constant need to blow my nose, I felt I would pass. It was very necessary to pass: I was convinced that this encounter would be our last, and that I had a good deal for which I should make amends. A good deal of irrational feeling and a good deal of halfheartedness. I was in debt, and I do not like to leave my debts beyond the end of the week.

When Wyndham arrived, I went to the door to let him in. The sight of him affected me strangely, for he looked more impressive, more rational an object of passion that I had thought. I was ashamed, as though in my own mind and for reasons of my own I had belittled and diminished him in order to keep him safe, when the real Wyndham had been carrying on all the time quite independently. He kissed me on the cheek and told me that I must get back into bed. Then he came and sat on my bedside chair, where the doctor had sat, and looked at me with his bedside manner.

"Poor Emma," he said after a while. "Poor old Emma. All that water. Did it feel very horrid? I should have jumped in after you, shouldn't I? I was just rooted to the ground."

"It didn't feel too bad. Muddy, that's all."

"God, you were quick off the mark, you were in there before I'd noticed what was happening."

"You couldn't be expected to notice. It's my job to notice. I'm always waiting for this kind of thing to happen. I wasn't even surprised, I knew it was coming."

"I've written to the garden people telling them to put railings along the water's edge. One of those little ones, about a foot high."

"Have you really? That was nice of you."

"Too late, though."

"Too late for Flora?"

"Too late for you and me."

"Yes, I suppose so. Though if it hadn't been that, it would have been something else."

"Yes. You'll have to spend the next few years listening over your shoulder, I can see that now, it was impressed on me very forcibly by that incident. Don't think I missed it."

"And David, too."

"Yes. David is necessary, too. To pick up the bits, eh?"

"Wyndham, I said, holding very tight on to the edge of my sheet and sitting bolt upright, as though facing a judge and jury, "Wyndham, I really must apologize. I had no right, no right whatsoever, to put myself in a situation where you might think—where you might expect— where I was any way committed to go through with it. When we began, I honestly thought I could. I wanted to. But there are more things stopping me than I realized, and I apologize for not having recognized them earlier."

"You weren't to know," he said. "I didn't know, I didn't see it that way myself until yesterday."

"But what else is there in my life? What else can I have?"

"You've got a good deal, haven't you? Anyway, you'll be able to go back to it when the children are grown up. In fifteen years' time they won't be falling in rivers, will they?"

"But I'll be so old."

"You won't be as old as I am now. And you're the kind of woman who'll look extraordinary at forty."

"But in fifteen years you'll be too old, even if I'm not."

"Oh yes. We'll be no good to each other then."

"I want now," I said, "I want now, I want now, I want now."

"Then you shouldn't have married," said Wyndham. "People who get married give up the here and now for the sake of the hereafter, didn't you know?"

"No, I didn't know."

"Well, you know now. Emma, give me a kiss."

"I don't feel like kissing," I said. "I can't breathe through my nose, I need my mouth for breathing."

But he came and sat on the bed and kissed me just the same, and put his hand down the front of my dressing gown and nightdress. For the first time I was not bound up with black lace and elastic, and I could feel something beginning to move inside my skin.

"You feel like a sparrow," he said, "you're all bones."

"I'm not bones," I said, and he pushed me back onto the pillow. We struggled there for a little, and after a while I began to think that I really might as well give in: there was, after all, everything on the side of submission and nothing to be gained by resistance except a purely technical chastity. For we are what we seem to be, and there can be no doubt about what I seemed to the world to be at that moment. So I let him get on with it, and I wish to God that I could say that I enjoyed it. At the end I looked around limply for my hand-kerchief; then, not finding it, blew my nose loudly on the corner of the sheet. Poor Wynd-ham lay there with his eyes shut for some time, till I began to think he had gone to sleep, and reached furtively for the thermometer; he open-ed his eyes to see me taking my temperature.

"Emma, " he said, "you're crazy," and shut them again. I did not blame him.

My temperature had not in fact risen. I be-gan to feel a little better, as though it had, as they say, done me good. I started to watch Wyndham, who was still lying there looking dazed. I stroked his hair a little, and then, to my immense surprise said:

"I say, Wyndham, whatever made them call you a ridiculous name like that?"

He groaned and turned over onto his side, away from me.

"My mother," he said. "My mother's idea, she was a great admirer of Wyndham Lewis. She met him once on a ship."

I nodded to myself, glad that that was set-tled. I felt that I was beginning to get things straight. I also began to feel a sort of brisk energy taking possession of me.

"I say, Wyndham," I said again, after a while, when I had mollified his exhausted, sul-len look by a little earnibbling and kissing, "would you like a cup of tea?"

He groaned once more, but I took it for assent, and went off into the kitchen to put the kettle on. I even started to sing to myself that selfsame ditty about *Oh yes, my darling daugh-*

ter that had been on my mind ever since Flora's adventure. While the kettle boiled, I started to tidy up the breakfast plates, which had not been properly dealt with. When I went back with the tray of tea things, Wyndham was sitting on the bed, fully dressed, looking a little less bearlike.

"Let's go and sit in the sitting room," I said. "It's a frightful mess in here."

"Are you sure you're feeling all right?" he said as he meekly followed me. "I should never have done that, I forgot about your being ill."

"I'm not ill," I said as I sat down on the settee. "I've never felt better. I am sorry, though, it must have been frightful. Me sniffing and all that. It can't have been much fun for you."

"Oh well," he said, "fun, that wasn't the point."

We sat and drank our tea, staring at each other. I remember that my hair, whenever it swung across my face, as it frequently did that afternoon, kept catching on the slight unaccustomed stickiness of my lipstick. There is something extraordinary voluptuous about that recollection. There was nothing else voluptuous about the situation at all: Wyndham and I sat there drinking our tea and eyeing each other in, I think, almost total ignorance of each other's state of mind. I knew that for me this was some kind of end, and I was suspiciously watching for any sign that he might think it was a beginning. I could not get over the bright superficial cheeriness with which I had reacted. I suppose it was simply a mixture of physical and mental relief, a sense of having survived, though not exactly intact, a threat that had been hanging over me for a long time.

At about five o'clock I looked at my watch and remarked that it was time he was going as the others might come back at any moment.

"It wouldn't really matter if they did, would it?" Wyndham said moodily.

"Oh yes it would," I said. "I'm supposed to have spent the afternoon in bed. I don't want them to come and find me up."

"We did spend some of the afternoon in bed," he said. "It was you that wanted to get up, not me."

"Oh well," I said, "that's not the point," and I got busily to my feet and started to stack up the teacups and pick up crumbs from the floor, indicating that I seriously intended his departure. It is striking and frightening, in recollection, to see how clearly, how childishly, how womanlike I take refuge in triviality and try to order chaos by sweeping up a few crumbs. He watched me heavily for a moment or two, and then he said:

"You're very house-proud, aren't you, Emma Evans?"

"House-proud?" I echoed indignantly. "Do you think so?" It was not a word that I associated with my own approach to decor.

"Well," he said, indicating with a sweep of the arm my pictures, my china, my lumps of marble and my scraps of velvet, "it's all very cozy in here, isn't it?"

"Cozy?" I wondered if he could be serious: the accusation seemed as remote as if he had suddenly said, "You're looking fat today."

"Isn't it cozy? All these bits and pieces? It reminds me of my aunt's rooms at Binneford, they were always full of stuff."

I said nothing. I stood there waiting for him to go. He stared up at me from the depths of his armchair, and I thought to myself, You're a fool, he doesn't know anything about you or care anything about you, he just wanted to get you into bed, and now he's seen what you are there, now he's seen the frigid, scrappy, icy core of the thing, he thinks that you remind him of his aunt.

This was what I thought, but I did not much care. I was shinily preserved from feeling. I was simply waiting for him to go. Finally he got to his feet and said:

"Well, Emma, I suppose I don't want to meet David after all, so you'd better get back to bed, and I'll be off. I hope I haven't given you pneumonia."

"Don't worry," I said, "I have a strong constitution," and I remembered too late that I had never told him about my mother, so that he was unfairly spared any real solicitude about my health. He advanced on me as though about to give me a dutiful parting kiss, but I flinched and swerved away and made for the door. He followed me along the corridor to the door at the top of the stairs, and there he said:

"I'll see you again before I go, shall I? I'm leaving at the end of the week."

"But you'll be back, won't you, during the season?"

"Maybe. To see how things are going. I'll see you again, anyway, before I go."

We were both suffering acutely from something like embarrassment; the uncertainty between us was growing obscenely.

"Give me a ring," I said quickly, to put an end to it: that foolish, perennial last plea.

"Yes," he said, "I'll give you a ring," and he went downstairs to his car, which he had driven right into the garage. It was the first time the garage had been used for its proper function since our arrival, and there was hardly room for a car amongst the junk. I followed him halfway down the stairs and watched him get into it. I felt as well acquainted with that car as I did with the man himself; it seemed as much a part of what had occurred as any more fleshy detail. Wyndham Farrar, Oundle and ENSA, who had an old maroon Jaguar car and a great weakness for braised celery. I leaned on the banisters and gazed at him intently as he looked in his pockets for the key. Now that he was safely out of reach I felt the dim beginnings of regret, for I knew that I did not know him, but that if things had been otherwise I could have loved him. Somewhere I had gone wrong; I had opened myself either too little or too much, I had not faced the choice that I should have faced and I had ended up with neither infidelity nor satisfaction.

He switched the engine on, then looked up to me and waved, a little plaintively. I waved back, and I could not for the life of me have said whether he was plaintive from disappointed passion, from disappointed lust or from a bad headache. He started to back towards the garage door, and I turned away and began to go up the steps, but just as I turned I heard him shout.

"Emma," he yelled, and I turned round, expecting I don't know what clarification, and he gestured and pointed towards the doors and said, "Come on down and wave me out, Emma, there's a good girl, I can't see a bloody thing round this corner."

I nearly retorted that I was in my dressing gown, but thought better of it and slopped down the stairs to him in my slippers.

"You should have thought of this," I said as I took up my position by the corner of the doorway. "You should have backed in."

"Oh yes," he said crossly, over his shoulder, "you think of everything, don't you. You're the one who never makes mistakes. Stop telling me how to drive, you don't know anything about driving."

And he started to back towards me, his eyes more upon me than on any signals about the traffic that I might be giving him. I looked out at the road to wave him on, and then stepped smartly in again when I saw a car that I took to be Neville's approaching from the distant corner. I turned to make some communication of this, and to try to get out of the way and up the stairs again, and as I turned Wyndham's car hit me: he was backing towards the left-hand side of the garage doors, and he got me just against the doorjamb with the rear left-hand wheel. For the first second I thought the car had just touched me, and then I thought that I was dead. I was pinned against the wall, unable to move, and the car did not seem to stop. For a very long time it moved in on me,

the whole weighty metal mass of it, crushing
my legs together and me to the wall, and then
I started to scream and the car stopped, leaving
me caught from the thighs downwards, and
not merely caught, but squashed and crushed
and flattened by wheel and mudguard. I went
on screaming as I realized what had happened.
Thoughts of amputation, of myself without
legs, began to flash across my mind, and I continued to yell as loudly as I could, from pain
and indignation. It seemed a very long time
before Wyndham got out and came to see what
had happened; he put his shoulder against the
car and tried to heave it off, but without success, and we had time to look at each other and
to wonder what to do. Speed seemed to be
necessary, but I could not think in what direction.

"Just get in again," I think I said, "and drive
it off, drive back into the garage," but it was
apparently not as simple as that because of the
way the wheels were locked and twisted; in
order to move off me they would first have had
to move farther in. I cannot remember what
happened next. I can remember the feel of that
car, and the feel of my kneecaps crunched together neatly on top of each other, but I do not
know whether I spoke or whether I continued
to make a noise or whether I was silenced. My
recollection is restricted to my knees. I do not
know what we would have done. Wyndham
was trying once more to relieve the pressure by
pulling the car off me with his bare hands, and
I was watching his efforts and trying to feel
whether my feet were still attached, when
Neville's car pulled up and David got out.

This must mean, if it really had been David that I had seen when I first went to the garage door, that the whole accident had taken an infinitesimal amount of time; but they say that time seems long to drowning men, so why not to a woman with her legs squashed by a car?

When David arrived things began to happen: he came running over, a crowd began to collect on the pavement and he and Wyndham and a man out of a baker's van managed to heave that huge monster of a thing a couple of inches off the ground, so that I could finally move. I stepped out, or David pulled me out, I forget which, and then I fainted.

I came round a few moments later, lying on my bed, to the sound of Wyndham telephoning for the doctor. David was sitting on the bedside chair. I shut my eyes again quickly and said:

"Don't ring for that doctor, send for someone different, please."

"Don't be silly," said David, and there was nothing more that I could do.

It turned out that I had not done anything really terrible to my legs, though it was a long time before this consolation was offered to me, and there was sufficient mess for me to worry for a good few hours about amputation. I had injured one of my kneecaps in a very nasty and painful fashion, and my legs from the thigh downwards were covered in the most appalling bruises I have ever seen. I think that they wanted to take me to hospital, but I would not leave the children. It was the same doctor, and when he came I cried and cried and kept saying that I was sorry, as though he really had been my father, and as though a moral error had been committed, discovered and punished. Throughout the day I could hear Wyndham and David in the next room talking about me as though I were dead. Wyndham kept saying things like, "I could never have known she'd have moved like that, but I should have been watching more closely. I admit I wasn't watching," and David kept saying, "It's not your fault, for God's sake, don't apologize, it's not your fault. She should have realized. It's not your fault."

It was nobody's fault but mine, it seemed: anyone else would have known how to avoid a backing car. I lay there sleepless, tossing and turning as much of me as I could turn, and remembering one of my nannies who used to say to me, "If you don't stop crying, I'll give you something to cry for." I had got it now, and it served me right. At midnight, when he got back from the theatre, David came in to see me. I was still awake, as I had not taken the sleeping pills which the doctor had provided. By the dim bedside light he looked haggard and worn, as though he, too, had been having a hard time. He sat on the edge of the bed and took my hand and started to stroke it, very gently, the fingers and the dry hollow of the palm and the thick tingling pad of the thumb bone. It was as though I had not felt him touch me for years. There seemed, on this occasion, no reason not to feel him, no need to hold myself back, no cause for flinching. After a while he said:

"I'm sorry, Emma, it was very selfish of me, I

didn't realize how boring it would be for you here. Or if I did realize, I didn't care."

"Oh," I said, "it wasn't that, it wasn't only that."

"It really was Wyndham then, was it?"

"Oh, I don't know. I don't know what it was. I don't know anything about Wyndham. He's gone now anyway, hasn't he?"

"Yes, he's gone. Emma, I'm sorry about Sophy."

"Oh, that's all right. Don't bother about that. Fair's fair. You had to have something, didn't you?"

"It seems we both had to have something. It seems that's how we are."

"I wouldn't mind, I wouldn't mind at all, but my whole life seems to be so trivial, David, just one domestic accident after another, just one mistake after another. Why can't I make things important any more, why couldn't I manage to make Wyndham important?"

"Wasn't he?"

"Well, not really, was he? He'll just go off to London now and find some other girl and fall in love with her and take her out to dinner and tell her lovely stories and get upset. I feel sorry for most people, but not for him, he's all right. And I don't care. Not at all."

"Yes. I daresay it's just about the same with Sophy. She's got her eye on Neville already, did you know?"

"Not really? I thought that Neville and Viola—"

"No, Viola's gone off him recently. Her fiancé came up last weekend, he's finished work on that film, whatever it's called, that epic thing in Greece, and she's gone right off Neville. Sophy's bloody quick off the mark, I'll say that for her; she may not be an intellectual giant in other respects, but she can smell a change of heart from a mile away."

"Do you think she'd have a nice time with Neville?"

"I don't see why not. I like him, don't you? I say, Emma, talking about epic films, do you know who wrote to me this morning? Rockie Goldenberg. They're doing some great sea thing in the East Indies, some story by Smollett, he said, and he wondered if I'd be interested in it. How would you like to go to the East Indies? It would make a change, wouldn't it?"

"I should think it's just like Hereford," I said, and started to laugh.

"Oh God, you're crazy," he said, and began to kiss my arm, and I lay there laughing and sneezing and saying, "I love you, David," for quite a long time, not particularly because I meant it or felt it, but because I knew that in view of the facts, it must be true. When I stopped, he said:

"What's so funny about the East Indies?" and I said:

"We'd all have to have injections; think of poor old Flora and Joseph, full of needles," but already my imagination was at work, I had packed our bags and written to the estate agents in Hong Kong, and I knew so well that David had done the same. We were cheered by the promise of this grand excursion as Flora is cheered after a fall by the offer of a sweet or a go on the swings. We had too much in common by now, David and I, ever to escape.

For the next few weeks I had to stay in bed because of the bruises and my kneecap. After the first day or two it did not hurt very much, so I had quite a pleasant time. Everyone came to visit me, and brought me presents, and I did not have to do the cooking. I had a much fuller social life than I had hitherto experienced in that ill-fated town: even Sophy came and sat by my bed and ate my grapes and chatted to me about her prospects and about Neville and whether she could afford six guineas for a very nice pair of suede shoes. I was kind to her; now that David was, as I sensed, in the clear, there was no point in being otherwise. I could see once more what I had originally seen: the infinite fragility of her aspirations. I could not help but give her the support and encouragement that she demanded, although at the same time I could see that she and those like her are not in themselves finally fragile, although a woman like me, wanting what they want, would be. But I, being different, and being what I am, am made for survival.

During those weeks in bed, despite my somewhat weakened physical state, I became increasingly aware of my own strength and of what a mistake I had made in trying to relapse into self-pity or the kind of romantic, self-centered indulgence that an affair with Wyndham had promised. These things had been against my nature and against my situation, and I had not been able to go through with them. The truth was that I could survive anything, that I was made of cast iron and that I would have to spend my life not in protecting myself but in protecting others from myself,

starting with my children, and continuing with
the rest of my acquaintance. Things could
come and things could go, but I was never
going to have a nervous breakdown: the most
they could do to me would be to squash me up
against a wall with a big car. I stopped worrying, for those few weeks, though I daresay not
for good, about whether I was frigid, or trivial
or hard. I just took it that I now was all these
things and got on with it. Although the truth
is, as I quite well know, that nothing is trivial,
there is a providence, as the Bible says, in the
fall of a sparrow.

Wyndham wrote me a letter. I was tremendously touched by it, for I think I had
never expected him, after all that secrecy, to
commit himself, even after the event, in writing. It had a charming literate clumsiness. Poor
old Wyndham, I think he is basically a sham,
he has all the attributes of quality without
quality itself, though I may well think that because I wish to think it, having lost him. And
do not underestimate me. Although I choose to
lose, I also choose that same word loss to describe my choice. Things happen, but not easily. Wyndham said in his letter that he had
been very unhappy on my account, and felt
very responsible for me, or would feel responsible if he did not think I could get on better
without him and indeed quite well without
anyone. He said that he was going to make a
film, and that Edmund Carpenter was working
on the script, and that he thought Harriet Peters was going to be in it; had I ever met Harriet, she looked a little like me, and like me,
seemed to live on *hors d'oeuvres*. He said that

he hoped my children were well and that he would never fall in love with a woman with children again.

I could see Wyndham dining out with Harriet Peters and telling her anecdotes about me. I was glad to have given him a little material. It was all the same to me, one way or the other.

The only person who did not come to visit me on my sickbed was Julian. I noticed this after some time, and finally asked David where he was. David looked green, and tried to put me off, and then told me that Julian had chucked himself into the river the day after my accident, and had been fished out two miles farther down. It appeared that the strain of deciding whether or not to continue being an actor and whether or not to give in to Michael Fenwick had proved too much for him. Indecision drowned him. I used to be like Julian myself, but now I have two children, and you will not find me at the bottom of any river. I have grown into the earth, I am terrestrial. It is hard in such a state, particularly when it is achieved through labour, to remember sufficiently and grieve sufficiently for those who are not; but it is necessary. In the case of Julian grief involved no effort, for I knew him and liked him. But the others must be thought of, too.

I have had a good deal of time for reading recently. I have read Wordsworth and Hume and Victorian novels, and other things. Hume sums it all up in one sentence: by the word "all" I indicate the subject, my marriage. "Whoever considers," Hume says, "the length and feebleness of human infancy, with the concern

which both sexes naturally have for their off-
spring, will easily perceive that there must be a
union of male and female for the education of
the young, and that this union must be of considerable duration." I like the way that Hume
slips in words like "naturally" and "easily"; he
reminds me of my father, disarming by the apparent mildness of his expectations. And the
phrase "of considerable duration" rolls round
my mind with the comforting logic that more
passionate descriptions lack. It answers all of
them, Mike Papini and Wyndham and Sophy
and David and the lot, and it reminds me, too,
of what Wyndham said, of the necessary pleasure of feeling from time to time the warm
sense of defeat. I have read Wordsworth also,
the early poems, those selfsame poems over
which I sniggered and jeered when seventeen
and brilliant at school: we were taught to think
them ludicrous, and at *The Idiot Boy* even
Mary Scott had laughed. But now I do not
laugh, I weep, real wet tears, the same tears
that I shed over newspaper reports of air
disasters, for they are as moving as air disasters,
those poems, they have as high a content of
uninflated truth. And I weep partly as an
apology for my past ignorance, from which I
might never have been rescued. Wordsworth,
and the sylvan Wye, which got Julian and
made a bid for my Flora. Time and maternity
can so force and violate a personality that it
can hardly remember what it was.

When they at last allowed me to get up
again, the season was nearly over. The summer
was about to fall, and the leaves had begun to
turn on the chestnut trees. To celebrate my

recovery we took Flora and Joseph out into the
country in Neville's car: David sang all the
way, "This is Flora's holiday." He sings very
nicely, being Welsh. We went up on Ewyas
Harold Common, just beyond Abbeydore. The
common is beautiful, all bracken and buzzing
creatures and sheep. We lay down in the brack-
en, David and Joe and I, and Flora rushed
around making the sheep run. She would dash
up to the poor dozy sacks of wool and wave
and clap her hands and yell "Baa-baa black
sheeps," and they would stumble to their feet
and shamble off. David and I watched her with
our usual painfully acute mixture of anxiety
and delight, and after a while Joseph, who had
hardly yet got round to talking, suddenly made
a loud sheep noise as well. We were overjoyed;
Flora came running back to admire her brother's new accomplishment, and Joe sat there
saying "Baa-baa" for hours. Had David and I
been two entirely different people, we might
well that afternoon have been entirely happy;
and even being what we were, we did not do
too badly.

On the way back to the car Flora dashed at a
sheep that was lying in the path, but unlike all
the others, it did not get up and move: it stared
at us instead with a sick and stricken indignation. Flora passed on quickly, pretending for
pride's sake that she had not noticed its recal-
citrance; but as I passed, walking slowly, sup-
ported by David, I looked more closely and I
saw curled up and clutching at the sheep's
belly a real snake. I did not say anything to
David: I did not want to admit that I had
seen it, but I did see it, I can see it still. It is the

only wild snake that I have ever seen. In my book on Herefordshire it says that that part of the country is notorious for its snakes. But "Oh well, so what," is all that one can say, the Garden of Eden was crawling with them, too, and David and I managed to lie amongst them for one whole pleasant afternoon. One just has to keep on and to pretend, for the sake of the children, not to notice. Otherwise one might just as well stay at home.

℗

Quality PLUME Paperbacks for Your Bookshelf